I0649707

ELENA ULANOVSKY

NEW APOCALYPSE

BOSTON · 2022

Elena Ulanovsky New APOCALYPSE. *A novel*
Translated into English by Isabel Quintana
Edited by Pilar Quintana
Copy-edited by Daniel Ulanovsky

Copyright © 2000–2022 by Elena Ulanovsky

All rights reserved. No part of this book may be reproduced or utilized in any form or by any means, electronic or mechanical, including photocopying, recording, or by any information storage and retrieval system, without the written permission of the copyright holder.

ISBN 978-1950319961

Published by M·GRAPHICS | BOSTON, MA
  🖥 www.mgraphics-books.com
  ✉ mgraphics.books@gmail.com

Book Design by M·Graphics © 2022
Cover Design by Larisa Studinskaya © 2022

Cover Art by Maryna Daykovsky and Pilar Quintana
Text Illustrations by Maryna Daykovsky
Author Photo on the Back Cover by Igor Shraybman

Printed in the U.S.A.

Dedicated to my husband Alexander Ulanovsky,
my parents Vita Aronovna and Mila Moishevich Miroshnikov,
my brother Alexander Miroshnik,
and my children, Misha, Katya, Danik, and Karina.
Without them, this book would not exist.

I express my sincerest gratitude to
Isabel and Pilar Quintana for their unprecedented
and sincere assistance with the translation
and adaptation of this book into English,
for the time and the strength of spirit they shared,
as well as for their moral support
throughout this long journey.

Elena Ulanovsky

Chapter One

THE SMALL PLAZA AT the port of Haifa was densely packed with people. An observer might have thought the scene peaceful, at first glance. Women and children waiting to board a cruise ship to Greece with their suitcases, trunks, and bags. It would have seemed so, if not for the oppressive silence—everyone, even the children, spoke in whispers—and the complete absence of men in the crowd. And the cordon of mujahideen with Kalashnikov assault rifles.

The Special United Muslim Corps brought to mind old Soviet films of the Russian Revolution in the Central Asian republics, with their exotic appearance, or, in more modern times, the war in Afghanistan. To Alina, the people gathered in the plaza resembled a crowd of Jews awaiting passage to a concentration camp. And even someone lacking her imagination would have had to acknowledge the similarity.

In truth, their reality was not so bad. If war could ever be considered "not so bad." Civilians were being evacuated from areas under the control of the mujahideen in accordance with an agreement with the United Nations. The actual conflict would begin afterwards. The whole of northern Israel, including Haifa, had been surrendered to the Special United Muslim Corps without firing a single bullet, in accordance with the same agreement, and by personal order of the President of the United States. The Israeli government had had no right to vote on such issues for years now.

The Israeli Defense Forces, consisting of all males from 17 to 60 years of age, were mobilized and stood near Tel Aviv,

9

just 60 miles from Haifa. As a result, the mujahideen were engaged in the evacuation of the civilian population in Haifa and the north.

Alina would never have left of her own free will, since she had two sons, a husband, and a brother in the army, and her father was in the civilian defense unit. But she could not sentence her younger children to life in a war zone, and so she had packed their suitcases.

Only women with children would be allowed on the first ship out. And you needed permission to board. Fortunately, Alina knew Louise, a Christian Arab woman who got a pass for Alina and her friend, Oksana.

Louise had founded a center to combat abortion on the premises of a former bar that specialized in "girls" for foreign sailors. That bar, once run by Gosha, an old friend of Alina's, was on the same block as Alina's former office. Louise's husband, Angelo, was an important port supervisor, and enjoyed some privileges in the newly-established regime because he spoke Arabic, although he was a Christian.

Louise and her two younger children—her eldest having been mobilized to civil service—were about fifty yards ahead, closer to the ship. She waved vigorously across the distance at Alina and Oksana, trying to get their attention. Alina furtively whispered something to Oksana, whose white fingers squeezed her son Davidik's shoulder as she listened and nodded. She was to remain with the suitcases.

Alina tore across the thicket of bodies and baggage towards Louise, her hands firmly clutching those of her children. These she would not let go of.

A few minutes later, she was listening to Louise's distraught whisper, peppered with Arabic words although she was speaking Hebrew. Angelo had managed to slip a note to Louise informing her that the Christian mission in Israel, the Russian Orthodox Church and the Russian Consul were being allowed to fly their constituents out of the county to Greece or Russia. Only Jews would remain here.

At this point Louise stopped, sobbed convulsively, and covered her mouth with a corner of her kerchief. Angelo had heard two high ranking officers from the mujahideen speaking amongst themselves with his own two ears. They said that the ship sitting placidly in the harbor before them—the ship they were waiting to board—would be blown up as soon as it reached neutral waters.

Turning on petrified legs, Alina looked back at Oksana, who waved the pink form that she had received from a guard across the distance. Louise held a similar form. Alina tried for several seconds to read the writing, but the script blurred before her eyes until she realized that the form was in Arabic. Louise translated, "Here, you see … this is my surname, this is my religious affiliation, this is the number of children under 16…"

The pink passes had apparently been done up in a hurry. The names of the children were not entered, only the number of children belonging to the parent. And … what a stroke of luck! The number was in Roman numerals. A clear II was entered on Louise's form. "Hold my bag," Alina said, handing her bag to Louise. Alina's mind raced as she began unbuttoning her blouse.

Louise watched her machinations with large round eyes, fully convinced that Alina had snapped. Without wasting time on explanations, Alina unfastened a pin in the lining of her bra—following in the footsteps of past generations—and took out a sack made out of a Kapron stocking held together with a safety pin. It held some gold jewelry—not royal pendants, of course, and not hereditary diamonds, but rings and earrings given to her by her lover, now husband, on her birthday and other occasions. She quickly poured out half of the gold trinkets and hid them in her pocket. She then took the now-lighter sack and fastened it with the same pin to the chain around her son's neck, removing the dog tag which had been hanging there with his name on it.

Alina stuck her hands down her jeans, pulled out a bundle of bills, and counted out two thousand dollars, which was exactly half of what she had. She slipped the money into a stunned Louise's hand as she took back her bag.

"Lastly …" Alina whispered. Reaching for a pen, she carefully added a line next to the number of children on Louise's pink "pass to live" so that it read III. "Ron will be your third child. I'm not asking for anything. Just keep him sheltered. Just keep him alive."

Alina put her son's little hand into Louise's. "Aunt Louise is your mother now until I return. Don't let them see that you don't know Arabic, because they'll kill you." She nodded in the guards' direction. "We will meet again soon."

Realizing that this was not the time to cry, Ron nodded seriously and bit his lip. Then Alina kissed them—Louise on both cheeks, and her little son on his forehead—and, lifting her daughter into her arms, she began to make her way back to Oksana. Only once did she turn around, to see her child against the background of her friend's Arab family.

How fortunate that she had decided to shave his head before school started, Alina thought. The top of his head was tan, and he was almost chocolate colored, having spent so many days with his grandmother by the sea. He had his father's bright blue eyes, but they were fashionably covered by the sunglasses— "like the pilots wear!"— that he had begged for when shopping for his school clothes. He sported a striking McDonald's visor, which came with the purchase of a giant hamburger. Ron also had his father's appetite. He looked just like Louise's son, and dozens of other children in the port plaza wearing similar outfits.

"Long live interculturalism and globalization!" Alina snickered, comforting herself that even now her sense of humor remained intact, as she bumped up against her own suitcase beside Oksana. Mashenka, still silently pressed to her cheek, coughed a thin, pitiful chuckle.

Oksana held her pink pass at arm's length as if it was a rattlesnake, and, furrowing her red eyebrows, struggled to make out what was written on it. "They shouted my passport number in English and my surname, and when I responded, one of the guards made his way here, thrust this into my hand and started to drag us out. I resisted," Oksana winced with fear and disgust, "so he quickly left me alone."

"Of course, he did," Alina grumbled bitterly. "He gets a couple of extra corpses."

"Corpses? What are you talking about? … What are you doing?"

Lowering her daughter to the floor, Alina had begun to take her remaining "treasures" from her pocket and unceremoniously shove them into Oksana's bra. She then took the dog tags off her daughter, and added an extra "I" to Oksana's pink pass. She patted Davidik's head. "Now Mari-Mashenka will be your sister," she said. "Take care of her."

Oksana was speechless.

"You're the minority," Alina explained, "the gentile. But lo and behold, justice will prevail. You get to fly to Russia on a special chartered plane. And we? … Kaboom!" Alina motioned an explosion with her hands.

Oksana was Russian, but she had married a Jew, whether because of her magnanimous nature, which rendered her incapable of prejudice, or perhaps because she had felt sorry for him, treated as a second-class citizen in his native Ukraine. In Russia, her daughters were considered Jews, because of their father, so immediately after perestroika the family decided to emigrate to Israel. Oksana did not want to leave her mother, as her father was dying. Nor could she bear to leave her sister, who had a disabled husband. But she had to do this, for the sake of the children.

In Israel, her daughters magically transformed from being Jews to being Russians. The dash on their identity cards made it clear that they were not Jews, since their mother was not Jewish. As Pushkin would have said, they were "not a mouse, not a frog, but some unknown animal." The IDF, however, accepted them willingly. So now her girls were soldiers, sitting in stifling tents on the Negev Desert, listening to the radio broadcast from neighboring Jordan. Fortunately, they had studied Arabic diligently in school.

But their mother had not even had a chance to say goodbye to them before this fateful day of separation.

"And what about you?" Oksana dropped to her knees and began rummaging in a suitcase. "Well, where is it? … Ah, here, found you!" She held something up to Alina. "You know I'm not a believer, and my mother isn't either, but my grandmother believed. She was from a remote place, Kostroma. This icon, according to her, protects you from death. Take it…"

"I'd rather have an explosion-proof vest…" Alina sneered gloomily.

Trying not to burst into tears, Alina watched as her daughter shuffled behind Oksana on her plump little legs, clutching at Davidik's hand indifferently, not even looking back, so confident was she that her mother would be there, as always. Only now did it hit Alina that she would probably never see her daughter's chubby legs again. But now that her children were safe, she could break away from here—break through the cordon, creep along on her belly if necessary—nothing and no one could force her to step on that suicide ship.

Alina began to make her way slowly to the plaza, which was fenced in with temporary wire. It was not barbed wire, thank God, nor was it electrified. But every twenty meters there was a guard behind the fence, with the desiccated face of an Egyptian mummy and a machine gun at the ready. Moving slowly along the edge, past the mujahideen spaced out like fence posts, Alina gradually lost hope of finding a loophole in the impenetrable man-fence.

In the midst of all this tension, Alina found herself contemplating the morality of fleeing when several hundred women and children were being led to slaughter, like a herd of cows in a slaughterhouse. She pushed the thought from her mind. What would she accomplish if she tried to warn the others of the fate about to befall them? The mujahideen did not know

Russian—there was no danger on that front. But the people—would they believe her?

It had always been difficult for Alina to comprehend how, in every Soviet World War II film she had ever seen, a mere hundred Gestapo—even armed— could force a crowd of thousands into death camps. It seemed that people, even when they knew what awaited them, obediently walked on, although they could have crushed their torturers with their sheer numbers if they had tried. And if their foes had used their automatic weapons on them? That would only have hastened their inevitable deaths.

But people believe in miracles, Alina thought. They believe they can get out of a bad situation. It's that simple. Alina herself did not intend to give up, although she had already walked almost the entire periphery. If she could get close to the ladder and slip into the water ... that might work. She could swim, after all...

She could picture the scene in an action movie: the main character in the water, automatic gunfire causing the water to burst in spots as it mixed with blood, the body of a beautiful woman bobbing up (face up, of course), her clothes clinging to her body, torn in all the right places... A very romantic death scene. Alina critically examined herself and sighed.

But no. Hollywood could not fail her today of all days. And main characters never die—this she had learned from her husband, a great devotee of thrillers...

At that moment, Alina noticed that one of the mujahideen "tin soldiers" near her was behaving strangely. In contrast to the others, he was looking very carefully at the women and children crowding in front of him, as if he were listening to their muffled conversations, which merged into a monotonous rustle, like the sound of the surf. He seemed to catch some familiar sounds, and he smiled with his eyes only. Then he whistled a touching, familiar melody. It couldn't be! Moscow Nights...

Alina pushed her way through the crowd to the guard. "You speak Russian? You studied in the Union? In Moscow?"

"No, in Kyiv..."

"In Kyiv!" Like all people from Kyiv, Alina forgot everything else when she heard the name of her native city spoken in a foreign land. "Where did you live?"

"On the steep side of Andreevsky Spusk…"

"Oh, my aunt lived on that hill! I remember in autumn it was impossible to catch the chestnuts rolling down… Yes … but there weren't any student dormitories there…?"

"I lived with a friend. We were going to get married…" The guard took something out of his pocket. It was a smooth chestnut, almost merging in color with the palm on which it rested. On the polished shell, the letter "A" was thickly scratched and, scarcely discernible, a heart pierced with an arrow.

"Her name is Ann?" Alina asked, choosing a name at random.

"No, Alona. And her hair was … how do you say it in Russian … like this chestnut … no, even redder."

"A redhead?"

"Exactly."

Their soft nostalgia was interrupted by a rude hail in Arabic. The mujahideen's face instantly became impenetrable, and his body stretched like a taut string. Alina looked back. Around the fence, behind the sentinel guards, a second chain was being stretched out to block in the area.

Alina glanced at her watch—they would be boarding in ten minutes. There was only one option now—to dive into the sea. She turned to the ladders behind her, trying to figure out how best to lose her jeans and sneakers, which would hinder her ability to swim, when someone touched her shoulder. It was the Russian-speaking mujahid. Looking around anxiously, he handed Alina a coveted pink pass.

"Take it," he said. "This person didn't show up, and I've been wondering who to give this to. So sorry."

"Do you know there's a bomb on the ship?"

The guard nodded silently; his dark eyes desperate. Only now did Alina notice how young he was, almost a boy, probably the same age as her eldest.

"What are you doing here anyway," she asked. "You studied medicine, probably."

"Yes, not that it matters. In Gaza there is no work, and in Israel they won't give me a job—the war. And because of this, Alona did not come with me. But we all need to eat… And my relatives were saying, 'don't you want revenge for a brother, for a nephew, for a neighbor?' My mother was against it, crying… I got shoved into a suicide unit. I was barely able to break out and join this mujahideen detachment. Here the chances of staying alive are better. Well, for a war…

"Now about this ship … come, I'll take you where they won't scrutinize the documents. If you get out quickly, maybe you can warn someone. There are twenty hours left."

He climbed over the wire and began to lead Alina through the crush of people. She fought to stay right behind him, practically shoving her nose into his thin back. Her liberation was literally two steps away when the ship's powerful whistle blew, and almost simultaneously she heard guttural Arab cries and the screams of women in Hebrew: "It's leaving. The ship is leaving!"

Alina turned and saw the strangest thing—the ship was sailing away from the pier without a single passenger. The cries and lamentations of the women and children merged into a desperate cacophony.

"Calm down!" Alina cried out, her voice breaking from the effort to scream. "Calm down! They knew; they knew everything! A terrorist attack was planned, and the ship was going to explode! It's a blessing that it left. This is your salvation!"

Her voice was largely drowned out by the noise of the crowd, but those standing near her heard. And Alina discovered the true strength of a crowd when people believe what they want to believe, when they refuse to listen to the voice of reason, because it contradicts their faith, their belief.

They turned on her—these women, exhausted by unmet expectations, who had just been deprived of any hope of delivering their children from the hell of war. They grasped for her

18

and hissed like wildcats, shouting that this must be some Russian mafia scam—after all, it was a Russian ship—and that Alina was trying to profit from the grief of others. That ship would take people to safety alright, but only those who could afford to pay more, in some other port, and the likes of Alina would get paid highly, and take the best cabins on the ship for themselves.

Her entire day had been a surreal ordeal, but through it all, Alina had never been as frightened as she was now. The young mujahid could not understand what the women were shouting in Hebrew, but he quickly assessed the situation and fired off a short burst into the sky. Alina was certain that if he had not, the distraught women would have torn her limb from limb.

Her relief was short lived, however, and she found herself brought abruptly back to reality as the mujahid pulled her pink pass from her hand.

"This pass won't help you anymore," he said. "They've announced that everyone, without exception, will be taken hostage. In a few minutes they will start transporting everyone to a temporary camp. But," he concluded, "it's better than having taken off on that vessel." And turning, he took his place in the line of soldiers tightening around them.

Alina looked around. The women, now hushed and exhausted after the hurricane of emotions they had experienced, and their long list of fruitless expectations, had settled on the ground, or sat on their suitcases. The children mostly sat on their laps. It was almost peaceful, but Alina was sad. Now that the worst of the danger was over, she regretted parting with her children. What would she say to her husband, and where would she find them? She remembered stories she had heard of hostages taken by Muslims. She realized that any "happy ending" was still very far away. So she comforted herself with the thought that the decision to send the children off with Louise and Oksana had been the right one—no matter what the consequences.

Chapter Two

THE HOSTAGES WERE BROUGHT to an abandoned school. It was empty like many public buildings and private houses in Haifa. Almost all of the Jewish population had "got up and left," having learned that the city would be handed over to the combined Muslim detachments. Whoever could had gone abroad to stay with relatives. Those who couldn't leave had moved to the tent camps which had sprung up around greater Tel-Aviv.

The streets of the city were empty, as if a neutron bomb had exploded. Only in the Arab part of the city was there some glimmer of life. Yet even there, Israeli Arabs had mostly left the city to wait out the hard times with their relatives in the villages away from the turmoil, fearing the mujahideen more than the Israelis.

Alina stood at the window of an empty classroom, where the desks were perched one on top of the other along the walls, and mattresses were dumped in the center. The hostages were brought in by two elderly Arabs, the first Alina had seen that day without guns, who were probably quartermasters.

Ironically, Alina found herself at the school which her older children had attended when they had first arrived in Israel. And the building they had lived in stood nearby on the opposite side of the street. She remembered how, over ten years earlier, in the same dense yet empty dusk—they had said that the next day a war would officially start—their taxi, having circled for almost an hour along the narrow streets of Haifa, had finally stopped. And the swarthy driver had sighed with relief, having finished an endless dialogue with the dispatcher in an incomprehensible language that she had yet to learn.

In her new apartment, rented from someone who she later discovered was a drug dealer, there were two remarkable sights: a metal front door with a small window (apparently for dispensing drugs), and a pentagonal room with a balcony, the windows overlooking the sea. The next day she had put on her gas mask amidst the howling of the sirens. Alina now remembered how the first thing she had learned upon her arrival was that it was best to lay her children near the inner walls during a bombing, because the external walls were the first to be destroyed when a bomb hit. And yet, there was the view of the sea…

That building, which she had not visited since that time, was associated in her memory with yet another war. A friend of Yoram's, an old acquaintance of Alina's who had fought in the Haganah in 1948, had told her that it was this very street that had been the front line, the border between the Arab and Jewish parts of the city. His younger brother had died, wearing a backpack full of explosives, when he had gotten caught in a crossfire of searchlights, and was taken out by a sniper on the roof of her house. And that boy was killed at eighteen… Where were her soldier sons?

Alina commanded herself to immediately stop her reminiscing. This was not the time for sentiment, but the time to return to her reality. As if in response to her thoughts, a very real, booming female voice behind her said, in clear Russian, "Come on, move! It's bedtime for the children. What do you think, that we women will be carrying these mattresses ourselves?"

The voice seemed familiar to Alina. She turned … of course, it was her old friend, Marina. A large woman, with wide hips, she deftly maneuvered between groups of people on mattresses, despite her size, while simultaneously commanding the two elderly Arabs. Not understanding a word, and being in fact the ones in control, they nevertheless obeyed the blond fury unquestioningly, removing the desks near the window. Either they had their own special instructions from their superiors on this score, or they simply felt they had to respect such a beauty.

Spotting an empty corner, Marina, rejoicing at seeing Alina, pulled Alina to her side and enjoined her to make this space their own. Two children, literally clinging to Marina's skirt hem, followed them. One was a fair-skinned girl of about 11, and the other a swarthy-looking boy, around 6, which was the age of Alina's son. As the classroom was already filled with angry women and children— who were willing to fight tooth and nail for a better spot in the room—Alina pulled Marina's children to herself, and gently stroked the girl's cheek. The girl had her mother's eyes, but the smile and her oval face came from her father, Victor.

Victor was charming. He had had many entanglements with women, and he always came out on top. But now that he was with Marina, he let her take the lead. Alina was glad that Marina had someone now. Although Alina knew that the girl was Victor's child from a previous relationship, the boy, in all likelihood, was their son. Their older children were, of course, also in the army, like Alina's. Alina tried to talk to the little boy, but he was wary and silent.

"Do not try," the girl suddenly said, "he doesn't know Russian, and his Hebrew is pitiful. He has just arrived from Romania and is afraid of everyone."

"I see," Alina replied, and didn't press the issue, as if children arrived from Romania on a daily basis during this war. Marina approached, having won her battle for territory in the classroom. She solemnly showed Alina a rather cozy corner of desks and mattresses, enclosed by suitcases, near a window.

"You seem to be settling in for the long haul," Alina smiled.

"For a long time, for a short time. It doesn't matter. We will live as people, no matter how long we have to sit here," Marina answered, as she gathered her luxurious blond hair into a ponytail. "As for the children," she continued, "they have to have the best."

"Yeah, the very best!" Alina couldn't resist using sarcasm as she looked at the classroom around them.

Those who had been able to capture decent spots were already going to sleep, and the losers, among whom Alina would certainly have been if she hadn't met her old friend, snapped at the others, who were demanding that the lights be turned off.

Alina glanced at the walls—flyers, drawings—an ordinary school. And in the middle, a huge poster, all scribbled in and painted with congratulations to the teacher, whose portrait was in the center, along with her birthday, exactly a month ago. Alina automatically made the calculation in her mind— the teacher was a Scorpio.

"Well now, tell me, where are your children? Why are you alone?" Marina, having settled the children on a mattress, poured some coffee from a huge thermos for Alina. Marina had always been the target of jokes among mutual friends for her resourcefulness and housekeeping skills.

In the past, when Marina had gone on picnics with friends, she had always managed to load her entire car with blankets, pillows, and other provisions. Her friends had mocked her for this because she had only had herself and her ten-year-old son with her. But now her tendencies had become advantageous.

The pseudo-idyllic scene was interrupted by guttural shouts in the corridor. The door swung open and a commander, sur-rounded by a retinue of translators and guards, made his first rounds.

The translator, shouting over the cries of newly awakened children, said that first they would search all suitcases and re-move mobile phones and radios, as no contact with the out-side world was allowed; second, toilet trips would be conduct-ed by only one mother and child at a time, and they would be accompanied by a guard; third, the windows could be opened, but it was forbidden to look out. In fact, guards were under command to shoot without warning if anyone loitered by the

23

windows. Any questions would have to be written down and submitted to a guard.

"Oh, now I feel like I'm in a democratic country," Alina thought sarcastically, "I could even invite my lawyer here…"

She felt a rabid anger at the prohibitions, and immediately wanted to escape at any cost. The anger kept her up all night, despite her fatigue. Since Marina could not sleep either, they talked all night while finishing the entire supply of coffee.

Marina monopolized the conversation. "Dana, as you probably guessed, Victor's daughter, has lived with us for five years. The girl is very attached to me, although at first it wasn't that easy between us. I refuse to marry Victor, so as not to make him too comfortable in our relationship. Every Friday he offers me his hand and his heart, accessorizing his proposal with flowers and gifts. And I keep him in suspense and refuse. I keep him on a short leash by keeping his focus on marrying me, instead of chasing other women. You remember how many he's had. For example, your sister…"

Marina threw Alina a knowing glance. Alina lowered her lashes, as pictures from her past came to her: her first meeting with Victor at her office, where she created astrological charts for her clients. He had come in hoping to learn about his fate, since he was entangled with two women. His chart had clearly shown the sign of an "unnatural death," which ended up being the death of his unhappy wife at the time. Then Dina, Alina's sister had passed. And perhaps now Marina? And, to be honest, her own short affair with this charismatic womanizer would count too, wouldn't it?

However, Marina and Victor had been together for five years, and nothing had happened yet. And this morning, Marina and Alina had miraculously avoided death during the terrorist attack. Maybe the stars were a little tired? Alina looked up.

"And this boy, Jonathan," Marina pointed at the young Romanian citizen, "could have been your son…"

Alina shuddered wondering how much Marina knew of the affair.

"Yes," Marina continued somewhat confrontationally, "you remember how that seventy-year-old man offered to support you and your endeavors if you married him, had his child, and signed a contract stating that you would never divorce him?"

Alina breathed a sigh of relief. She was talking about Yoram. "So, what happened to him?"

"Well, he went back to Romania, and now thrives there. In fact, he married a woman who bore him a child.

"A month ago, he decided to visit his daughters in Israel, and bring his son to meet his family. Well, he got into trouble! All of a sudden, one could not go back to Romania, as all flights were canceled. He discovered that women and children would be allowed to leave on this ship. So, he ran to me and put the boy's hand in mine, while shoving a stack of dollars in the other." Here Marina lowered her voice to a whisper, and absentmindedly ran her hand over her ample bosom, checking for the treasured package. "Then he ran to sign up for the civil defense squad. Who needs him there, tell me?"

"And how do you communicate with the boy, in what language?"

"This is how I communicate," Marina answered, gently stroking the sleeping boy's cheek. Her face brightened. "We find a common language."

Alina averted her eyes as her throat tightened.

"Why are we only talking about me?" Marina exclaimed suddenly.

Alina briefly described all that had happened to her that day, ending with her getting the pink slip too late.

Marina jumped in, "When I heard my name and passport number, I was too frightened to answer." Marina sighed, her dismay rising as she glanced at the sleeping children. "To think they would have been sleeping in the Hotel Russia—would have been in Red Square—if I hadn't been so overwhelmed this morning. I wasn't going to step forward for anything. I know what these people…"

"You should be grateful that you didn't board the ship." Alina understood now whose pink pass the mujahid had thrust at her. After all, the ways of the Lord are inscrutable.

"Okay, let's go to bed. It's four in the morning. Tomorrow, or rather today, will be a busy day. Listen…" Alina began to read out the schedule which had been distributed to all the prisoners during the authorities' visit. "Rise: 07:00. Food: three times a day. Wash: from 14:00 to 17:00, one person at a time each room. From 17:00 students from madrassas, accompanied by translators, will visit the cells—oh sorry—the classrooms, and give lectures on the topic "The Role of Islam in World History." This place will be a regular country club!"

Alina had made up the lectures to see if she could cheer Marina up a bit. But Marina, annoyed at herself for having lost the opportunity to be away safely with her children, in Moscow no less, had already turned to face the wall, pretending to be asleep.

Chapter Three

A FEW DAYS PASSED WITHOUT incident, and more importantly, without hope. They got used to going to the toilet with a guard, and washing their clothes by hand, a piece of soap in a washbasin, always from 14:00 to 17:00. They got used to complete isolation from the outside world even more quickly.

What was impossible to get used to was the fact that they could not get past the door, could not look out a window. "One false move and we shoot." True, no shots had yet been fired, but one tried not to give them a reason.

There was no lack of food though. In fact, Alina felt like a goose being force fed. A diet even seemed in order. The food was homemade by Arab women from the villages with the freshest produce. Rice with lentils, pita bread, hummus, olives—everything that was served during peacetime in Arab restaurants and considered a national delicacy. The violence having just begun, the country only recently isolated, no one was scrounging yet. One time, a basket with tangerines was dragged in, spreading the nostalgic aroma of New Year's Day throughout the classroom.

"But the New Year is in three weeks," Alina calculated. "Will I need to spend it here, while all of Europe, decorated with lights, will celebrate?"

Then Alina remembered that a week ago—the last time she had heard the news—the situation in Europe was not festive at all. A year ago there had been a terrorist attack in Britain, and the entire royal family had been targeted. Only the prince's daughter had survived, and she had become queen. For half a year she dealt with her grief and trauma with the help of doctors and psychologists. But then, shocking the entire country, she announced that she was marrying her longtime lover, a billionaire from Saudi Arabia, thus surpassing the late Princess Diana.

A month before the date of the August marriage was announced, a new prime minister was elected in an entirely democratic process—a second-generation citizen of England, the son of Pakistani immigrants, educated at Oxford and fervent in the Muslim faith of his ancestors, with which he identified.

In Germany, the Muslim party, which now represented the majority of the populace and held two thirds of the Bundestag, had put forth a presidential candidate. In Belgium and Holland, terrorist detachments, covertly subsidized by Kuwait and Saudi Arabia, seized public buildings and held several hundred hostages in them. So old Europe stood on the threshold of great changes, and could no longer complain of boredom or satiety.

Eastern Europe, on the other hand, remained surprisingly calm. However, the Arab republics of the former Soviet Union, where since time immemorial millions of Muslims had lived, participated in the process of global Islamization.

In America, as always, terrorist attacks were acts of saber-rattling and mad shouting about revenge, with no real enemy to face on a battlefield. The time-worn strategies of armies landing, fighting, finishing the battle, and dispersing were useless now.

Alina was brought out of her reveries about world politics by a dispute between two women whose children refused to share a toy. Almost imperceptibly, and somewhat annoyingly to Marina, Alina had gotten to know everyone in the classroom. Her energy bubbling in the absence of her children, she found herself reading her new acquaintances' horoscopes in an effort to dispel the tension of their confinement and uncertain future.

So she approached the disputants and announced that, as an official astrologer, according to the way the stars were aligned the toy should be given to that girl. She pointed to a child on a mattress near the front door. The children calmed down instantly, brightened, and ran to the girl to get acquainted. However, the girl's mother looked dissatisfied with the attention.

This woman had not made contact with anyone. She had entered the classroom last, and taken a spot near the front door, demanding nothing more, despite the fact that she had not only a five-year-old but also a baby. She opened her shirt and fed her baby, laying herself on the mattress and pulling both children to her, as she had done every day of the entire week.

Alina remembered her as Rita, her children's teacher. She remembered having struggled to explain something to Rita in broken Hebrew, while Rita listened with angelic patience and made as if she understood. Alina had not known that Rita was from a Russian family and could easily have switched to Russian; but she had chosen not to demean Alina, and instead had given her the opportunity to feel equal to the other parents.

Rita noticed Alina's gaze. "Yes," she said in fluent Russian, "the irony of fate—to have worked at this school for 17 years and now be a hostage—a hostage of this school and a hostage of fate…"

At this mysterious turn of phrase, Alina recalled that for the last few nights, when Alina had gone to the toilet more often than the others, hoping to study the situation and perhaps to meet the Russian-speaking mujahid, Rita's spot had been empty. The girl was there sleeping, but Rita and the baby were not.

Alina returned to her mattress in thought. Somehow, she felt in her gut this was connected with an opportunity to get out of this prison. Perhaps Rita knew some loophole. After all, it had to count for something that she had worked at this school for so many years!

Considering the various possibilities of this latest development, Alina quietly fell asleep. Rumbling, flashes of light, and children crying woke her with a start. "They started bombing!" flashed through her mind as she sprang to her feet. It turned out to be just a thunderstorm—real, natural and very strong. The wind shattered a window, the door banged on the wall, and splinters fell across the floor. Alina decided to check out the situation in the corridor and headed "to the toilet."

At the door, she glanced at Rita's mattress and saw the girl, startled from sleep and now crying. Rita was nowhere, nor was the baby. Alina sat on the mattress and began to calm the girl until she fell asleep again, her head on Alina's knees. When Rita eventually slipped silently into the room, she paused for a second, seeing Alina holding her daughter, but immediately caught herself.

"Thank you," Rita said. "If you don't mind, could you stay with her a little while? Maya's afraid of thunderstorms. I'll be back soon." With that she walked stealthily out of the room. Only then did Alina realize that Rita's baby had not been in her arms.

Chapter Four

THE FOLLOWING DAY ALINA stared at Rita relentlessly, almost demanding an explanation. By the evening, Rita surrendered. "I have to tell you something. Maybe you can understand." She tapped her hand on the mattress, inviting Alina to sit next to her. To be fair, Alina was a specialist at "understanding" people, and women especially seemed to sense it.

Rita began at the beginning, with her childhood. "My parents came from Tashkent. My grandmother was evacuated there from Kyiv during the Second World War... My father taught at Tashkent University—Arabic language and the history of Islam. He was one of the people who translated the Quran into Russian, and the languages of the Central Asian republics. In our house there were always scholars and religious figures from Iran, Pakistan, Egypt... I was as young as Maya at the time." Rita nodded in the direction of her daughter. "So young that I don't remember details. All these people in turbans and flowing robes seemed to me to be characters from One Thousand and One Nights, which were my favorite fairy tales. I grew up with a sense of respect and love for Arabic culture and the Muslim religion.

"We arrived in Israel in the seventies. Like the first buds of spring flowers, my father was full of enthusiasm. As a linguist he planned to be in academia... But everything turned out differently, not at all the way he expected. Here, Arabic studies didn't interest anyone in academia, due to the proximity of the subject. My father could use his knowledge only in practical applications: translations, decoding, listening, forecasting ethnic relations… He was taken to a military department, despite the fact that they didn't really trust 'Russians.' In the end, his sympathy for the Muslims, his ties and correspondence with his friends and colleagues from Arab countries, didn't serve him well. In short, he finished his career as simply a teacher of Arabic. However, he did not forbid me from taking his same path. 'The enemy must be known in person,' he sadly said.

"So I became a student at Tel Aviv University. Since I could read and write Arabic quite well, due to my father's efforts, studying Arabic was not difficult at all. I had plenty of time while at university. So I worked as a translator at all kinds of conferences and meetings, sometimes ironically for the same military department that my father had worked for.

"I needed money, since it was impossible, on my father's teacher's salary, to pay for my studies, rent an apartment, and well … to have a basic existence at all. My mother didn't work, as she had gotten used to being a 'professor's wife' in Tashkent. She was a real beauty. Maya looks like her." The girl, hearing her name, looked up at her mother with large round eyes in which one could drown. Rita smiled sweetly at her daughter.

"So my mother was beautiful, although she wasn't stylish, and she was terribly scatterbrained. In Tashkent, my father drove me and my brother to the store to buy clothing exactly twice a year—once in the 'winter' and once in the 'summer'—although in Tashkent, as you know, there really wasn't any difference. He took advantage of the trip to buy a couple of outfits 'for our mother,' as he put it, and this was our clothing allotment for the year.

"Mom didn't know how to cook either. We lived on processed foods. So when my father had to entertain colleagues from abroad who were visiting his department, women from the university would come, all dressed up in silk dresses, and very quickly they would create the most scrumptious dishes in our kitchen.

"Here in Israel everything stayed exactly the same—except that our status, and our income, declined significantly. As you can imagine, with such a father, and without my mom's beauty, I grew up 'bookish' as they say. I had no relationships with boys, and didn't complain, since I figured that was a done deal.

"But when I went to university, I met a guy, and we even got an apartment together, though I never felt warmth from him. I read about 'how a working woman should look good for her man' and took cooking courses, but he took my efforts for granted, and didn't protest when I paid for him when we went out. I've always had a job, but he, for some reason, could never find one.

"Then it happened that I was working as an interpreter for an Egyptian lawyer—such an unpretentious gray suit, so different from my heroes of One Thousand and One Nights. We always spoke purely on a professional basis, so much so that after the conference ended, I completely forgot what he looked like and would not have even recognized him at a meeting. So, I was surprised when the agency said he had requested me to translate for him again.

"At the end of the first day of our resumed acquaintance, the Egyptian asked me to help translate some documents in his room, and, as he nervously smoothed the moustache he had grown since we first met, which didn't suit him very well, he told me that I was the woman of his dreams, and that he had known it the first moment we met, but had doubted himself. Still, he insisted that since then all he could think about was me.

"On the one hand I was so flattered, but on the other hand I could not have been more insulted. What did he take me for? I was not an escort, but a translator! This I expressed to him sternly, emphasizing that we could only have a professional relationship and no other.

"The lawyer's face fell, but he apologized and escorted me to the door, and the next morning a fax came, stating that his company had refused my services and had terminated the contract. It was a big blow to my pocket, because it was a good contract—for an entire two weeks. I had even bought tickets to surprise my friend in Amsterdam for her birthday, and now I had to cancel the trip. But most of all I was stung by the lack of consideration of my professional skills, of which I was very proud.

"A month later, out of the blue, the lawyer called and asked my forgiveness for terminating the contract. He said he was returning to Israel for business and needed my services. 'Just for work,' he emphasized.

"My financial situation that month had greatly deteriorated. Forget the trip to Amsterdam. It was now about trying to support my family. My father was diagnosed with a serious illness and needed money for an operation, as well as money just to survive, because he could not work anymore either and was not old enough to receive a pension yet. My mother wasn't going to get any retirement. This meant that I was going to have to take a break from school to work, despite the fact that I only had one semester left to graduate.

"So, of course, I agreed and was ready to translate around the clock. The client remembered to keep his promise for the first two days. On the third day, the harassment began. There were declarations of love in a heated whisper, and then he groped me against a wall. I struggled and ran home, but the following day I returned, as I really needed the work.

"Two weeks passed. Then one day we were returning from Yafo, along the seaside highway, and the lawyer turned onto a deserted beach. Once again, he began to profess his love for me, while running his hand up my skirt. I stopped resisting.

"'Now,' he said, choked with feeling, 'I am the happiest man in the world. I realize that you love me too.'

"And the funny thing was … that he was not far from the truth.

"My friend at the university, having sensed that things had changed, had finally begun to show a serious interest in me, even offering me his hand and his heart. He had already secured a position as a military translator after graduation, and that was a stable job, a good salary… Dad had to have an operation, followed by another operation. So, I, of course, had agreed. Love and marriage were not connected in my mind, especially since Khalid (that was the lawyer's name) already had a large family in Cairo.

"He came to Haifa every other month for one week, and we spent a lot of time together—'working.' And so, a few years passed…

"Strangely, even with such a vigorous sex life I couldn't get pregnant, until my husband and I tried artificial insemination, and Mayechka was born… And this one" she continued, looking at the babe in her arms, "then made his own appearance—my little Arab."

Love stories across boundaries had always fascinated Alina… "Yes, but how," Alina asked, "is this connected with what is happening here?"

"What do you mean 'how?' Khalid. You saw him. He's the commander here."

Chapter Five

ALINA WAS SHOCKED AND about to barrage Rita with questions when a mustached translator appeared at the door. "Don't get ready for bed yet," he announced. "The commander will be making rounds with some people soon."

Alina returned to her corner, knowing that Marina would be in a panic about the rounds. Marina's face lit up to see her friend return. "Who's that?" she asked, rolling her eyes towards Rita.

"She taught me Hebrew in an adult second language program. We were just gossiping about my classmates—who is where now, what they're doing."

The door opened again, and the commander entered the classroom, as always, with his retinue. "Wow, Khalid," thought Alina. She now looked at the commander as if seeing him for the first time. He was no Hollywood star, and yet he was not as homely as Rita had described him. Or did his military uniform (to which Alina, like most women, was not indifferent) make him more interesting? She was so carried away that she didn't realize that Marina was elbowing her in the ribs and hissing, "Look, look! Don't you recognize him? That's Gosha, your friend!"

Alina looked closer. Indeed, standing behind the commander was Gosha, the former owner of the sailor's den, and a supplier of carnal entertainment for the famous in the city.

He had stopped that line of work before the war—Alina remembered his tragic past, like a film flashing through her mind in fast forward—and had then opened up a music school for gifted children.

The translator introduced Gosha as the mayor of the city of Haifa, who had come to check the conditions in which the hostages were being held. "If you have any questions, complaints, or suggestions, you can express them to the mayor."

Hearing this, Marina, with unusual speed, grabbed Alina by the hand and dragged her until they were face to face with Gosha in the middle of the classroom.

"We have a very important message," Marina began, "but we want to speak with you in private, and are requesting this in front of the commanders." Marina glanced at the commander solicitously. The translator translated, and the commander nodded his ascent.

Seeing this, the other women began to shout out, crying, making requests. The noise surrounded them. The face of the commander was masked, but Gosha was visibly pale.

"All requests must be in writing," the commander finally said, and the delegation hastily retreated.

"What do you plan to tell them?" Alina asked Marina.

"What does it matter? You're smart. You'll come up with something. We needed to make sure Gosha saw us."

Alina was once again struck by Marina's strong survival instinct, but did not have time to object as a mujahid guard entered the classroom and silently pointed them in the direction of the door. Accompanied by the security guard, both women strayed for the first time in many days from the familiar route of classroom to toilet. As far as Alina could recall, this corridor led to the principal's office.

Khalid—Alina could not get used to the fact that the commanding mujahid had a name, like any normal person—sat at the director's desk, buried in papers.

Not even honoring the newcomers with a glance, he pointed uceremoniously to the chairs set aside for visitors, in one of which Gosha sat. Two mujahideen stood at the door to the office. The translator sat the hostages down next to Gosha and pulled up a chair beside the director's desk. To Alina's great relief, nobody asked the dreaded question: "What was so important that you asked to see the mayor?"

Speaking in Hebrew, appearing generally quite at ease, Gosha told Alina and Marina that he had run for mayor because he was inspired by his own success in teaching music and aesthetics to future generations.

The irony of his destiny was that he had been elected two months ago, just as the war had begun.

Gosha continued, "And now men are being drafted and mobilized, women are evacuating with their children, and I am stranded, as the captain of the ship who cannot leave his post. I go every day to an empty city hall building and I stand alone, guarding over the interests of the city: watching for loiterers, making payments to repair crews to keep the water and gas lines operational... So, I came here—the soul who shoulders everyone's burdens..."

"Gosha," Alina said quietly in Russian, noting that the translator was momentarily distracted, "I need to go to Moscow. I sent my daughter there with strangers, and I have to find her. I know that the airlines aren't running right now, but your sister has a charter company in Moscow, right?"

Without changing his posture, and keeping his expression completely neutral, Gosha answered in a placid tone. "If you can get out of here, I will get you to Moscow. Once a week a plane leaves from Haifa. You know my address. I'm always home after six pm these days. Phones, of course, won't work. You'd need to make it to my house. But I can't help you get out of here."

Alina turned away in despair ... and noticed the mujahid who stood two steps away guarding the door. He was the man who had tried to save her at the seaport. He, of course, had heard everything and understood everything. Alina was at wit's end, not knowing whether to laugh or cry.

Later in the evening, in a whispered discussion of the grim events of the past day, Alina and Marina managed to laugh a little, remembering how Gosha couldn't take his eyes off Marina's shapely thighs, barely concealed beneath her knitted skirt, which was practically painted on. Marina had borrowed the skirt from Alina, although it didn't fit, because her own clothes were hanging on the corners of desks drying. So much for her industriousness in getting all her laundry washed.

When everything was quiet in the classroom, and even Marina had finally begun to breathe evenly and deeply, Alina lay awake, miserably pondering her escape. A slowly widening strip of light from the door to the corridor suddenly caught her attention. Maybe Rita needed help. Alina quietly rose from the mattress, carefully trying not to step on anyone's outstretched limbs. She moved to the door and quietly looked out, and suddenly found herself face to face with her almost-friend from Kyiv.

"What's your name?" was the first thing that came out of her, unexpectedly.

"Dzhabril, and you?"

"Alina."

"So, Alina, I heard everything. I also want to go to Moscow. From there, Kyiv is not more than a day by train. I will meet with my girlfriend, Alona, and I will live like a human being."

"But Ukraine is not the best place to live."

"But it will not be necessary for me to act like a guard dog, keeping women and children hostage. And tomorrow, perhaps, they will force me to shoot, and the day after tomorrow they will strap a backpack with explosives on me—and goodbye… "

"So, help Marina and me get out of here. Somebody promised to help me… "

"We need to find another exit door. We can't leave through the main door."

"I will try to find out tomorrow. You be here tomorrow night at the same time."

Alina returned to the room. Rita and the baby weren't there. Maya slept restlessly, shifting and sometimes sobbing in her sleep. Alina lay down next to the girl to wait for Rita, and quietly fell asleep.

Rita didn't return until the morning, so Alina had to postpone the conversation she wanted to have with her until the evening.

"Listen, I need to get out of here," Alina whispered to Rita when it got dark and everyone had settled down, "to find my children! Only you can help me."

"Khalid will not do anything," Rita wrung her hands in fright. "If he helped you, he would get the death penalty! And he has already committed high treason because of me…"

"What do you mean?"

"Do you know that the ship at the port was going to be blown up in neutral waters? A relative of Khalid's, an engineer—who studied, by the way, in the Soviet Union—participated in loading the explosives on the ship. Got big money for it.

"Khalid learned of this plan two days before the boat was set to depart. He said that he almost lost his mind with fear, knowing I would be on that boat. We had agreed to meet in Greece even before this, because of the war. He had rented an apartment for us. The tickets had been bought. Then last week, while he was still in Egypt, I was here with the children. The last few days I hadn't lived at home, but with a friend whose husband was in the army. She had sent her parents to her relatives in Ashdod, and she felt safer with some company.

"So when Khalid heard of the bombing, he quickly realized that he could not find me. I was waiting for the plane to Greece to take off in a week. He put an anonymous letter at the Russian embassy in Cairo because the ship was a Russian ship. If he had been caught, it would have been the death penalty without any trial! You know, Egypt doesn't stand on ceremony when it comes to treason. And then he enlisted in this squad, trying to get here and find me… "

"Wait," Alina interrupted her. "He doesn't need to be compromised! You've worked here for so many years. Where is there a back door? I will arrange the rest myself."

"There is an exit in the gym. It is not far from the toilet, to the right along the corridor about a hundred meters, then to the left. You need to pass through the gym. Then in the far-right corner is the door. It exits directly onto the street. Only it's locked. I'll get you the key in the morning. And now I'm leaving. Please lie down again with Maya tonight," Rita looked at Alina pleadingly, although Rita was already rising to her feet.

Alina got up quickly after she left, expecting Dzhabril to be just outside the door, which he was. She quickly told Dzhabril her plan and turned to leave, but he stopped her.

"Wait, not so fast. We need to check the key first—it may not open the door. Also, on the way there is another room with a guard on duty. He may be interested in where I'm taking women, especially if they do not return. So you need to wait until my friend is on duty. He won't question it. And finally, on the way to the gym there is a staff room for the teachers, which has been adopted by the mujahideen. This is probably not the best way, even at night. Don't rush this."

Returning to the classroom, Alina settled on the mattress near Rita's daughter. It was impossible to try to sleep… Despite the seeming simplicity of her plan, the escape was still very risky. Whereas with Khalid, the situation was not atrocious yet. If they stayed it was possible to at least stay alive, as they say. Perhaps it would be better to wait?

Alina was sure that the authorities would not leave the hostages to the mercy of fate. She had heard that among the captives there were several wives and daughters of high-ranking government members along with their children and grandchildren. There was even a journalist from the New York Times here, who had imprudently come to Israel to visit her grandparents.

The women had collected money and gold to pay a mujahid who had agreed to pass on information via the internet about the reporter who was a hostage to her parents in America, hoping that they would get some international publicity.

So why should Alina take such a risk now? Was it justified? Indeed, if they failed, they would be executed... The mujahideen would stop at nothing. After all, one person more or less... On the other hand, if the skirmishes started again, the chances of surviving here would decrease to nothing... Millions of people would die in the flames of war, wouldn't they?

And then her children would be left alone in this cruel world. Even if they survived the war, thanks to friends, in some quiet, remote location, their souls would be permanently mutilated by the tragic loss of war and becoming orphans. No, Alina would not sit and wait for the wheels of history to turn. She had to get out of this camp and act defiantly, as her maternal instinct was telling her to do.

The arrow on the wall clock crawled to four. Rita would come soon. She always returned before dawn. Alina realized that today she would not fall asleep. She rolled over and allowed her thoughts to roam. And another reason occurred to her that disallowed her to remain inactive—her husband, her beloved.

Despite the fact that their family life was mature, calm and safe, their romance had not lost its freshness; and Alina still thought of him less as her husband, and more as her lover. She had put so much effort into this love that she could never forsake it now. She remembered his hands, gently tucking her hair behind her ear (how he loved to see her face), his slow, cautious movements and almost weightless kisses.

Of course, she promised herself. The first thing I'll do when I leave here is to try to see him—whatever it takes—to calm him down before I depart. Love, for her, was the only thing of value, and for its sake, she would take any risk.

Rita snuck into the class, tiptoeing. Her eyes, alight with happiness, glittered even in the diffuse light of dawn, as if confirming that Alina had made the right decision.

Holding the coveted key in her greedy palm, Alina moved to her mattress and lost herself in a short dream, having decided to inform Marina about the escape in the morning, since they couldn't pack anything but their documents anyway. "This will be tragic for Marina," Alina thought to herself, as she fell asleep, picturing her friend with a large, stuffed suitcase.

And sure enough, in the morning, Marina panicked. "How can we leave without anything? What about the children? In Russia, the winter. Okay, wait, put the warm things in a basin, as if we were going to wash them."

Having spent the whole day on pins and needles, Alina finally handed the key over to Dzhabril, who was where he said he would be at the appointed time like clockwork. He returned an hour later and gave the go-ahead. Trying not to think about what could happen to them if they failed, Alina took Dana's hand ("one woman, one child" was the toilet rule), and propping a basin on her hip, headed for the door. As she passed Rita, she leaned low and whispered, "Get ready. In 15 minutes Marina will follow with her son. Then it's your turn. You have half an hour."

"I'm not going anywhere. I'm with Khalid and my children every night. Nothing else interests me. Even if a bomb went off, I'd stay. Go, you wouldn't understand."

Alina smiled in gratitude for Rita's help and slipped out the door. She did understand, but now was not the time to tell her…

Everything went like clockwork, and within half an hour the small group consisting of two women, two children, and two washbasins, accompanied by an armed mujahid, exited the doors of the gym and were free.

Where to now?

"Wait a second," Dzhabril said, disappearing into the darkness. From somewhere came the sound of broken glass, then the rumbling of a running engine. After a few moments, a small green Fiat rolled up. The children were laid in the back seat and covered with clothes. Marina squeezed in with them, and Alina sat in the front. Dzhabril positioned his Kalashnikov in the broken window. After all, a soldier taking some girls for a ride, what could be more natural?

Alina could not hold back her curiosity. "How could you do this so quickly?" she asked.

"You forget where I grew up. When I was a child, assembling, disassembling, and stealing cars was like a sport. As a teenager, I worked at my uncle's garage. He sold the stolen cars for parts. We did what we had to do…"

Fifteen minutes later they arrived at Gosha's villa. Alina pressed the bell several times, but no sound came from behind the door.

"Maybe you got the address mixed up?" Marina asked nervously.

"Not likely," muttered Dzhabril and, breaking the window with the butt of his gun, he deftly pulled himself up and slid inside.

Ten minutes later, the entire company was settled down in Gosha's living room. Gosha was slowly recovering from the horror of waking up suddenly to find an armed Arab shaking his shoulder and quoting a famous Pushkin poem, in good Russian, no less: "Get up, wake up, beautiful! Open your shut eyes!"

In the end, having ascertained who was who, Gosha protested when he learned that the whole group was going to Moscow. "You are crazy! I'd have to buy half an airplane! Where would I get so much money?"

Alina was perplexed. She hadn't thought about money at all. But since she had given her money to Oksana and Louise for her children, she did not have a penny left. Marina spoke, "I'll pay. Just send us. I'll loan the money to everyone else."

"Another thing," Gosha's voice gradually acquired its usual pragmatic tone. "You cannot stay here. They'll miss you at the school, and with whom did you last speak? Only with me. And that's too coincidental… So you'll go to the Haifa airport. There, in the hotel, I have booked a room for you, not in my name…" Marina and Alina looked at each other, as they were aware of his previous occupation. "I don't know how you will fit in there. There are only two beds in the room…"

"No problem. Let's do it." Marina didn't flinch, despite her usual mores.

"Let him," Gosha nodded towards Dzhabril, "buy some food for you. He can shop in the Arab markets. And the day after tomorrow at 8 AM be ready as I'll come for you. The flight will be at ten. Get your cash ready, since no one will be accepting credit cards," Gosha joked, having recovered from his shock.

"Gosha," Alina hesitated. "Only one request… I must see my husband before I go."

Gosha interrupted her. "Don't even start. I understand that you want to see your husband, but there is no way to connect with Tel Aviv. All roads are blocked. There is no way to get there."

"So, I can get to Moscow but I can't get one hour away to Tel Aviv?"

"There may be an opportunity. I will forward your message, but I can't promise anything."

Chapter Six

"LISTEN," ALINA LEANED TOWARD Dzhabril, taking advantage of the fact that Marina was distracted by the children, as they drove to the airport. "I can't fly away without seeing my husband. You have to understand. I only need to get to Hadera, which is where the Jewish border is. Gosha said so."

"No problem," answered Dzhabril calmly. "Just let me get in touch with my mother first. She will find clothes for you. In the morning, she and my brother will take you through our posts as far as Hadera, and there you're on your own. Remember the plane departs the day after tomorrow at ten. We'll be leaving the hotel at eight that morning. My mother and brother will pick you up tomorrow night at the same place where they left you.

"Leave yourself plenty of time, as you never know what will happen. And don't get carried away, because the plane will fly away without you." He looked at Alina without a smile.

"But why bother your mother? I feel bad for her."

"Why? Why … to avoid them thinking of any conspiracy. Nobody will pester an old woman. And I want to send her to my relatives in another village, further away from harm."

Miraculously, Dzhabril managed to contact his mother, as the woman was afraid of answering the phone at night. She was informed that she would pick Alina up at the hotel at five in the morning.

A young Arab woman with tired, red-rimmed eyes greeted them in the hotel lobby. She was apparently both the manager and the night porter. After reading Goshe's note, she gave them the keys with an imperturbable expression, paying no attention to the motley crew before her, and not asking about the sleeping arrangements in the small room. It was evident that she had probably seen even worse.

After the crowded conditions of the classroom—the noise, the stuffiness, and the smell of unwashed bodies and baby diapers—this tiny hotel room with two beds, which were covered in clean linens and pink bedspreads, and with night lamps on the bedside tables, seemed like a luxurious paradise.

Alina insisted that everyone go to bed quickly, thereby curbing Marina's instincts to lay everything out and arrange her nest. After waiting for some time, Alina nudged Dzhabril, who was curled up on the floor, and began to dress quietly. From the next bed, Marina's unexpectedly wakeful voice said, "You're not going anywhere. I heard your so-called plans in the car. You're putting everything in jeopardy!" Marina then became outraged, and her whisper became a whistle. "Not only might you miss the plane, but you might die from a thousand ridiculous accidents! Leave your orphaned children to strangers. What kind of a mother are you?! No smelly pig is worth it!"

Dzhabril laughed, admiring the flowery curse. Alina had nothing to say. Marina was right. Yet it meant absolutely nothing...

"You know what?" Alina went all in. "Please, lend me two hundred dollars."

"Never!" Marina cut her off. "Maybe the lack of money will sober you up."

"Okay, don't fight," Dzhabril conciliated. "There you are, Alina. A hundred should be enough for one day."

Alina hid the money in her pocket and went to the door. When she was already at the threshold, Marina jumped towards her and put tightly folded bills in her hand, whispering passionately in her ear, "You fool."

Dzhabril and Alina went out into the street, and Alina breathed in the air of freedom. Despite the smell of fuel from the nearby airport and the aromas of the industrial zone, this morning could not be spoiled. The slow break of day with its cool freshness and sudden clarity of light was like a promise. Today promised Alina luck—good to start the day early.

Finally, Dzhabril's brother drove up in an old scratched Subaru. Outwardly he was the opposite of his brother—small, with a balding patch on the top of his head despite his youth. He looked very much like his mother. And he was smiling.

Their mother was sitting next to him—a plump woman with the kind face of a Ukrainian peasant, brown as if deeply sunburnt from harvesting potatoes.

Alina, receiving an armful of clothes, looked helplessly at Dzhabril. He shrugged and told her to put it all on, on top of her clothes. It's good that it's December and not July, thought Alina, as she put on a gray robe and squeezed into the back seat. Tying a headscarf on, she gave them the sign to proceed.

They reached Hadera in an hour, passing a dozen road blocks where they mercifully were ignored. Leaving the last block a safe distance behind, they stopped on the side of the road.

Climbing out of the car, Alina couldn't think of anything better, so she bowed to Dzhabril's mother, and shook hands with his brother through the open window.

"Wait," Dzhabril's brother said in Hebrew, "don't take your dress off. Walk along the roadside until you get to the border. The Israelis won't shoot a woman, even if she's an Arab. And when you approach them, you can explain everything. If you accidentally meet one of our patrols, move quickly, and if they stop you, lower your eyes and don't answer, as if you're shy. They won't touch you, especially so close to the Israeli border. We'll meet here again at eleven tonight."

Alina moved uncertainly along the edge of the road, concentrating on not stepping on her robe, until she heard her native tongue. Then she screamed in Hebrew, "Don't shoot! I'm looking for my husband." A minute later, she was pulling her robe over her head.

Following protocol, she was taken to their commander, where Alina stated the platoon assignments of her sons and husband, and asked to see them, as she was flying to Russia in the morning. Noticing the surprised looks on the faces of the soldiers—everyone knew that civilian flights from Israel had been shut down for a month—she added with importance, "at the personal invitation of the Russian consulate, on their plane."

Trying to give her due respect, the commander put her in an army maintenance truck headed for her younger son's unit. Trying not to fall asleep from the rhythmic lumbering of the truck, Alina mused.

They were very different, her boys: the eldest, Dmitri, was a clever man, philosophical, but clumsy as a bear cub; whereas her younger son, Andrei, was a womanizer and jack of all trades who worked as if his hands were on fire. The boys were great friends, and always found their common ground. Only once did they raise a wall between them—after her divorce, or better said, after her new marriage…

They both reacted to the appearance of a stranger in their house negatively, bristling like hedgehogs with their sharp quills raised. Dima even refused to come home from the army for visits, while Andrei tried to find some resolution to the untenable situation.

Those were very difficult days, but perhaps the most important of their shared history, because at some point the men realized that the happiness of someone, they loved was more important than their own egos. And the appearance of one, then another, charming baby sibling finally reconciled all to the situation. After all, who could resist the cute, cuddly creatures who climbed onto their laps, tried to pry off the badges from their uniforms, looked into their eyes and babbled something like "Favorite Dima!" Or "Andryusha, kiss…"

Her mind thus preoccupied; Alina didn't notice when they reached the base. As she exited the truck, she was hit by a sudden fear that perhaps Andrei had been sent on assignment somewhere. But no, here he was in his jeep, as always clean shaven and meticulously dressed. Due to his mother's arrival, he had been given a dismissal. His jeep was like a carriage at her disposal.

She didn't want to embarrass him with exaggeration or tears, so after a brief hug, they continued to Dima's unit. It turned out that it was not far, and Andrei visited him often. The elder son, unlike his younger brother, was thrifty, not spending money on clothes or girls. He didn't even know how to approach girls. He received a decent salary though, since he worked as a programmer, which was his specialty.

In fact, the one hundred dollars that Alina solemnly handed over to each of them was a ridiculously low sum for them, especially now, when, due to the economic isolation of the country, prices had jumped so high that it would only buy you three bottles of beer and two packs of cigarettes.

The boys' mood was excellent. There was not a hint of war in the air yet, but if something started, it would be even more fun for them. After all, anything would be better than the stagnation of the army base. They hadn't known what had happened to their mother, but felt sure that she and their younger siblings were completely safe with relatives in Arad.

Trying not to frighten them too much, Alina briefly described her adventures, as she needed to explain to them why she urgently needed to leave the country.

Dima was soon called back to his unit. Alina kissed him as if they would see each other again tomorrow, and, looking at his familiar lumbering walk—which he'd had even as a child, and was painfully reminiscent of her first husband—she convinced herself that nothing bad would happen to him or to Andrei. Why? Because it simply couldn't happen. Period.

Andrei was already beeping the jeep's horn, which emitted a melody instead of a honk. He announced that he would take her to her husband, who served an hour's drive away in the Ariel region; and, since he would be in the vicinity, if she was not offended, he also would stop and visit a couple of acquaintances at the adjacent bases. Bouquets, Alina noted, had already been bought and were neatly laid out in the back seat.

Her husband, unlike her sons, knew everything, except that his children were scattered around the world, and that Alina was no longer a hostage. After Andrei's call, he couldn't function, and stood at the entrance to the base, fraught with excitement, waiting for them.

Having dropped off his mother, Andrei hurriedly drove off, waving at her and shouting that he would return at nine at night.

Once, when he was explaining to Alina the principles of creating Hollywood films, her husband had said that directors avoided shooting scenes of real happiness, because acting it was almost impossible. It would have been impossible to capture the joy of their meeting now. It was always like this, after they had been separated; but this time their separation could become permanent.

In their joy there was bitterness, and excitement for their children, and fear of their upcoming separation, knowing that when they would next meet could not be determined, and might never be…

At eleven that night, Alina once again stood in the appointed place in a baggy Arab robe. When ten minutes had passed, and the Subaru had not appeared, Alina knew something had happened. There was no way to find out exactly what had happened, since she didn't know Dzhabril's mother's phone number and she didn't speak Arabic. And it was no use calling Marina, since the hotel phones were simply turned off.

Alina had no choice but to walk, avoiding military posts if possible and avoiding anyone spotting her. She couldn't stop any cars, or speak to any passersby. The only languages she knew well in this land were the languages of the enemy. Alina wandered along the side of the road, picking up her hem, and enviously recalling how deftly the Arab women moved in such garb in the market in Nazareth. Silently she tried to calculate how long it would take her to get to the Haifa Airport, remembering a fourth-grade textbook where she had had to calculate pedestrian speed.

Behind Alina, there was a rustle of tires on the side of the road. A jeep with the headlights turned off approached her. Alina felt her insides shrinking. It was pointless to run, as she would fall over in a minute, encumbered as she was by this prehistoric robe. Yet, if she had been in a tracksuit and sneakers, would that have helped? Only one thing remained—to face the danger.

The jeep stopped but did not turn on the headlights. Two Arabs got out, dressed in civilian clothes, looking like such thugs that Alina's tears flowed. Having a rich imagination, she had imagined similar situations many times—where she, helpless, faced people who were not people at all, and became a victim of violence in a split second—and here her imagination ended.

Alina stood looking down at the ground and dropped her hands helplessly. The Arabs stopped a stone's throw away. Then the eldest, shining a flashlight in her face, pulled a piece of paper from his pocket and, illuminating it with his flashlight, read with the intonation of a robot from a sixties film, "Are you Alina?"

Tearing his eyes from the paper, he waited for her affirmation, then continued to read, "Dzhabril ordered you be taken to the hotel. We are his friends. Do not be afraid." Alina looked at the paper streaked with Arabic writing. Apparently, Dzhabril had dictated to them the words in Russian, and they had written them out phonetically. Alina wanted to kiss their mustached snouts, which suddenly seemed so cute, but decided not to take any risks. Instead, she nodded with dignity and said "Shukram" (thank you), the only Arabic word she remembered. Which turned out to be the most appropriate word.

Dzhabril met Alina at the entrance to the hotel and explained that Khalid, having discovered the escape of the guard, had turned to the military police, who had sent troops to Dzhabril's family's home to conduct a stakeout. Dzhabril happened to call his brother to check in, and miraculously his younger brother had answered the phone immediately and been able to warn Dzhabril covertly, despite the troops being stationed there.

When Alina returned to the room, Marina pursed her lips and turned away. Well, her friend's discontent couldn't spoil Alina's sense of victory mixed with sadness... Everything had worked out for her. However, her separation from her husband and sons was not less painful now, and the future was no less foggy.

When the stubborn woman, facing the wall, finally fell asleep, Alina quietly asked Dzhabril what had happened during her absence.

"I think something went wrong with Gosha." Dzhabril said with a knowing look in his eyes. "He came to the hotel when I was out looking for a phone. What with the troops and all, an hour passed before I was able to ensure your safe return, and when I returned, the door to the room was closed. Nobody opened when I knocked, and I had no choice but to sit at the door and wait. I dozed off and woke up because Marina was shaking me and trying to drag me into the room. Gosha was no longer there, and the children were sleeping... "

The next morning, after a good night's sleep and a shower (there was a shower in the hotel—a great achievement of civilization!), Gosha came to pick them up. Alina decided that nothing had happened between Gosha and Marina, because she knew that Gosha's modus operandi was to treat women poorly after he had slept with them, and Gosha was looking into Marina's eyes ingratiatingly, while Marina joked with him, treating him carelessly, even slightly condescendingly...

Thinking about Marina and Gosha helped relieve the tension of the pre-flight anxiety that had seized Alina since entering the airport. The departure hall was packed with armed mujahideen, but the "letters of safe passage," as Alina jokingly called the documents signed by the Russian ambassador, and obtained by Gosha, worked flawlessly, magically opening all

doors. No one seemed to pay attention to either their citizenship or their religion.

Here they were, Russians in their bold duplicity, Alina thought. On the one hand, they blew a mountain of smoke, going off about how they were going to fight the Arabs; on the other, look how closely they worked with them... Only Russian planes were allowed to land at this airport. It was all for the sake of money, since the weapons the Russians sold to the Arabs were used to crush the opposition—who were not the strangers they might seem... After all, they were their former fellow citizens.

But Gosha—Alina glanced at her friend, reclining in a hard chair with his eyes closed—Gosha, of course, was a Russian spy. Otherwise, how could he have such power and freedom? But even if he was the devil himself, with horns on his head, all that mattered now was what he had done for her, and for all of them.

And Alina, overwhelmed with emotion, suddenly threw herself around Gosha's neck.

Chapter Seven

THEIR CHARTER PLANE LANDED at a small airport twenty kilometers from Moscow. Alina had been in Moscow seven years earlier when she had studied astrology there. The subsequent years had added new features to the appearance of the capital—one stylish boutique had been replaced by another, several huge American-style supermarkets had opened, and a couple more skyscrapers had grown in the center of the city.

But Dzhabril and Marina, who had not seen Moscow since the beginning of the "Big Aliyah," the mass Jewish Russian emigration in the 1990s, were struck by the changes. It was a different city than they remembered, with newfangled European trends, intermingled with the Belle Epoque period of Gilyarovsky's Moscow. At the same time, the capital was still Moscow—with its bridges over the partly frozen river, its spacious avenues, the warm breath emanating from the metro stations, which they remembered from their youth, the all-familiar spire of Moscow University, and St. Basil's Cathedral on Red Square.

The first thing they did was to drag the children to Red Square, after stopping at a flea market to purchase some warm clothes to wrap them in, the Italian sheepskin coats being too expensive to even consider. The very next day they flew to Kyiv, paying a huge sum for Ukrainian visas and plane tickets.

In Kyiv, Alina brought Marina and the children first to a hotel by the train station where she instructed her friend to buy tickets to Ternopil. Then they called Oksana, who lived in Ternopil, and who couldn't believe that Alina was calling from Kyiv. Masha, Alina's daughter, was fine.

Then Alina and Dzhabril went to see Alona, Dzhabril's long distance girlfriend on St. Andrew's Descent. Alina had noticed that he had not wanted to go alone, and she knew that her cousins had once lived nearby, her aunt having died long ago, and reasoned that it would be nice to revisit the streets of her childhood.

Alona was not at home. They knocked for a long time until a sleepy neighbor peered out of the adjacent door.

"Why are you knocking? She hasn't lived here for a long time. She married another dark one," she gestured to Dzhabril, "either from Algeria, or Iraq, left with him and is long gone. For a year now, if not… And what do our girls see in them anyway? True, they say they're great in bed," the neighbor winked at Alina vilely, not realizing that the "dark" man understood her.

"You know what?" suggested Alina. "Let's go to St. Cyril's Church. There is the famous icon of Our Lady there."

Soon they stood in front of the iconostasis, looking into Vrubel's depiction of the virgin's huge eyes.

"Religion is the opium of the people," Dzhabril quoted, affecting the voice of a lecturer on the subject of "scientific communism."

"I don't know though," Alina intoned, "I just don't know… Here we are in Kyiv, safe and sound, instead of being fish food at the bottom of the Mediterranean. Someone took care of us…"

Having lit a candle for those dear to her, regardless of their religion, Alina called Marina at the hotel and asked her to get another train ticket, for Dzhabril.

"Yes, done," muttered Marina. "I just paid for a whole compartment. The little one didn't need a ticket. But I was thinking, for forty dollars I don't have to endure a local with a snack of greasy bacon, and dirty socks."

That night on the train, after Dzhabril and the children went to sleep, Marina, properly warmed up from a few glasses of Gorilka, a traditional Ukrainian liquor, told Alina what had happened the evening before they departed, when Alina had gone to see her husband in Tel Aviv.

"Gosha showed up when Dzhabril left to make a call, and before I figured out what was happening, he had locked the door from the inside. He got pushy, telling me that he had fallen in love with me the first time he ever saw me—remember when I worked at his bar for three days? Of course, I immediately put a stop to his talk. Then he began to whisper gruffly, since the children were sleeping, that if I did not agree to be with him, he would not put me and the children on the plane tomorrow, and not you or Dzhabril either.

"But you know me. He can't take me on. 'It's not necessary,' I told him, 'I am okay here with the children. Why should I tumble around the world? I will live here. You won't turn me over to the Arabs. You don't have the guts. As for Alina, with her craziness and carelessness, her children are safer with strangers for now.'"

"Thanks a lot," retorted Alina offended.

But Marina didn't even honor her remark with a response. Instead, she continued. "I told him, 'as for Dzhabril, with all his romantic nonsense, you think I care? That's all of us. So, what are you going to do, huh?' Then Gosha, realizing that I wasn't going to be intimidated, began to tearfully complain that I couldn't imagine how hard it was for him; that after his friend Victor's mistress, Irina, was stabbed instead of himself, he became almost impotent; that apparently Irina had cursed him from beyond, because he could now only sleep with his wife, and then with difficulty, because she had never aroused in him any excitement; and that, after many years, I was the first woman to make him feel like a man again; and that now he was standing in front of me, dying of desire for me, and I had to help him.

"Well, I'm not a little girl, and he has done a lot for us… I helped him out a little… And then, you can't imagine, he fell to his knees and started kissing my legs, and told me that he had never really loved anyone in his life, despite the many women he'd known, and only now, in his old age, was he honored blah blah... Basically, what didn't he say? I can't even remember everything. I barely got rid of him. And that's when I noticed your guy," Marina nodded towards Dzhabril, "sleeping by the door."

Entertained with conversation, the first night on the train passed quickly, but the following day the train stopped at each station along the way. They traveled a distance with a view of steppes and copses of trees, in some places covered with snow—huge distances which Alina had long ago found familiar but which were now foreign. They spent a long time waiting for a taxi in the dank wind in front of the station building, and a long time searching through the streets for Oksana's old apartment building, which was completely covered in ice and didn't have a single lamp lit.

Marina had immediately left the train for her parents', promising Alina that she would join her for dinner tomorrow, with Dzhabril, Oksana, and, of course, Mashenka. She'd bring Jonathan as well, who would consider it a treat.

And now they were standing in front of the door to Oksana's apartment, and Alina did not dare to ring the bell. Seeing that she couldn't cope, Dzhabril pressed the button. The door swung open, and on the threshold stood ... Oksana, only 15 years younger, with the same red shock of curly hair, blue eyes, and creamy skin. Alina figured it must be Katya, Oksana's sister. Coming from the depths of the apartment, she heard children laughing and a cheerful ruckus...

Hearing Masha's voice, Alina ran into the room without removing her coat, grabbed the child in her arms, and pressed her to herself, inhaling her sweet, still-infant smell with sheer pleasure. At first the girl did not understand what was happening and pushed her mother away; and then, recognizing her mother, she burst into tears and cried for over twenty minutes. No one could calm her down.

"This the first time she's cried since I took her," Oksana said, and to prove it added, "ask Davidik."

Later in the evening, having put the children to bed and settled down to tea in the kitchen, Oksana confided that the month she had spent with her family had been difficult. First her father had died of a stroke. Then a week later Katya's husband, who had been ill with cancer for seven years but had not stopped drinking and tormenting his entire family, died. It would have seemed that they were free of him, but it was still a pity—a living soul gone…

Oksana had found out on the news that the ship had not picked up any passengers and that the explosives had been removed. So, she knew Alina was alive, and had been waiting for Alina's call a long time.

The situation in the world was terrible, but America was constantly negotiating with the Arab countries, and God willing there would be no war. Misha, Oksana's husband, had called from Israel; and David, Oksana's lover, had also called. Here Oksana glanced at Dzhabril, almost betraying her discomfort at being discovered with her furtive glance. Her children were fine. Alina's husband had also called yesterday, and knew that her flight was safe. Someone had told him, someone he didn't know … some "Gosha." Oksana looked inquisitively at Alina, but Alina dismissed her with a wave, not having the strength to go into it.

The next day they gathered to go visit Marina. Dzhabril flatly refused. First, he was fed up with Marina, with her bossing him around like an army sergeant, and secondly, he had promised Katya that he would fix the closet, since there were no men in the house.

Alina only now shamefully realized that because of the thrill of seeing her daughter and the joy of talking with Oksana, she had lost sight of the fact that Dzhabril was among complete strangers, and she had not paid him the slightest attention. However, noticing how intently Katya was explaining which cabinet door didn't close well, Alina realized that she needn't have worried.

Upon closer inspection, the woman who was so similar to Oksana with her red hair and blue eyes, was still different from her older sister. She was a little shorter and stockier, with a rounded face and snub nose. She would have been a jovial talker if she had not had an unbearably hard life.

She had gotten married at 16, unexpectedly for everyone, including herself, having gotten pregnant by a friend, who was only two years older. Together with the baby, Katya had gotten saddled with a husband who was like a character from a classic Russian novel, in that he drank, and having drunk, would beat anything that came close to his hand. In the intervals between drunkenness, he was gentle, caring, even gallant—a model husband.

And in this hell, Katya had lived for five years, during which time she gave birth to a second child. She had comforted herself with the delusion that she could divorce him if the situation got "very bad." But what "very bad" was, neither she nor anyone else could figure out.

To top it all off, during a routine physical examination at the plant where her husband worked, the doctors had given him a disappointing diagnosis—stomach cancer. The disease had only angered him. He hadn't stopped drinking. In fact, he continued selling anything valuable in the house to keep up with his habit; and what little they had left now had to pay for his medications also. Katya had sometimes found herself thinking that his death would be a relief, but then the shame of even thinking such a thing would have her sobbing for a week, mourning her husband's ruined life, as well as her own.

Dinner at Marina's was like a meeting of a military council. Her mother laid the table and then sat frowning by the window, listening to the names of unfamiliar cities and distant lands, only occasionally uttering, "Lord, have mercy."

Lord, have mercy—where had her daughter gone? Although she had been wayward and independent, having grown up without a father, she should still have been her mother's support. But where had she ended up? And weren't many of her friends, who had remained, just as well off as she? They had clothes and shoes. They didn't starve.

But no, her only daughter, her own blood, had taken off to distant lands; and, if not for this incomprehensible war, they would not have seen each other for another ten years. And she had seen her grandson, Timosha, only once, when he was five years old, and now, he was a soldier in the army. "Lord, have mercy, for I know how much my daughter worries about him."

Marina was really courageous, but Tim occupied her thoughts constantly, although his name was never uttered. In order not to rub salt in her wounds, Alina didn't mention that in that one short day in Tel Aviv she had managed to see not only her husband, but also both of her sons.

Victor, Marina's partner, took up much less space in Marina's worries, or maybe she was simply embarrassed to talk about him, or was trying to maintain the image of an independent woman. Oksana also had obvious (her husband and daughters) and secret (David) worries, but Alina and her friends didn't speak of these things. Alina herself thought only of Greece, where Louise, her children, and Alina's child were now.

She did not have accurate information about the political and military situation in Greece. The only thing she had accidentally heard on Russian television in the Moscow hotel was that the Turks had launched an assault by sea, taking advantage of the tense international situation, and had tried to capture the two largest Greek islands—Rhodes and Crete.

In addition to the book, Myths of Ancient Greece, which Katya kind-heartedly brought the next morning from their local library (both sisters read voraciously, as if trying to escape reality), there was an article about Greece in an old issue of Around the World magazine. In that article they mentioned that in Lviv there was a Greek Orthodox Church as well as a Russian Orthodox Church, although most citizens were Catholics.

Marina immediately called a friend of hers who lived in Lviv and ran a small stall at the Russian Orthodox Church there. A Greek friend was instructed to contact her colleagues in the Greek Orthodox Church and try to find some information. Meanwhile, Alina tried all day in vain to call the Greek embassy in Kyiv.

As always, the solution ended up being simple. The ubiquitous Marina remembered that her classmate, and first love in school, was now a manager in the shipping company that owned the ship that had been in Haifa that fateful day. It was rumored that the ship had sailed to Greece. Rumors were confirmed. "Vitenka," Marina gently purred his nickname into the phone, forgetting that she had called him at home. Victor told her that after the ship had been cleared it had traveled to Ashdod, although he had no idea where that was. Anyway, it later arrived safely in the Greek port of Piraeus with a group of Christian refugees from Israel, who were handed over to representatives of the Greek Orthodox Church. They were then taken by bus to Athens, to a hotel named the Divan Palace.

The information was accurate because Victor's son was a crew member. At this Marina rolled her eyes—my God how time flies! And he remembered the name of the hotel because it struck him as very oriental, and not Greek sounding at all.

This news cheered everyone up, and the fact that Victor didn't know where the port of Ashdod was bewildered the three friends. They, like native Israeli women, considered Israel a major Western power, like America, and it was simply embarrassing not to know where the main port of such a county was.

The last country of interest to this "military cabinet" was Romania, where Marina had promised Yoram to bring his son, Jonathan, when she had frivolously counted on the fact that closer geographical proximity would facilitate the task. She had not thought that, in wartime, even a distance of 100 kilometers could separate people for years.

But now, it was precisely because of Romania's strategic position on their "military" map that they solved the problem of how Alina and Mashenka would best get to Greece. It would be ridiculous for Alina to travel alone with her child across Ukraine, then fly to Moscow and have to pay again for visas. It would be much more convenient to get to Athens through Romania, since Ternopil had weekly flights to Bucharest, and Bucharest had daily flights to Greece. This plan helped Marina as well, since Alina suggested that she would bring Jonathan to his mother, and then Alina and Mashenka would have a place to stop. And so the group devised their strategy.

The week in Ukraine passed quickly. Alina had never visited Ternopil, but for some reason the provincial city seemed almost native to her, despite the fact that the architecture of its central buildings had elements of Catholic Gothic which was closer to Polish architecture than to the eighteenth-century classical style of Kyiv's architecture. Maybe the weather, which was nasty, with wind, wet snow and ice, reminded her profoundly of her girlhood home.

Putting on every single warm article of clothing that she owned, as well as Oksana's warm clothes, and wrapping Mashenka (who was affectionately known as Marika here) right up to her nose, Alina wandered the city for hours, reveling in the winter air, until the dank damp made its way to the very tips of her fingers. Then she went to one of the many cafés with Hutsul hatchets on the walls, unwound the many scarves around herself and her baby, unfastened their jackets and warmed herself with hot tea.

Hugging her huge cup with cold fingers and blowing on the steaming drink, Alina quietly watched her daughter and listened to her stories that Davidik was naughty, but not greedy; that Aunt Oksana drove them to the movies and there was all this shooting in the movie, and this film was not for girls; that Aunt Katya painted her nails with blue varnish, and this was not the same as that of adult aunts—red—and Davidik was jealous…

The serious face, golden curls and bright blue eyes came from her husband. Only the slightly almond shape of her eyes came from Alina. Alina's roots were one hundred percent Semitic; even the chief rabbi of Haifa, when preparing her documents for the chuppah, said that such purebred Jews are an invaluable gene pool and the pride of the Jewish nation.

Her daughter had grown up so much in this difficult month. Maybe it was true that one grew up quickly in hardship, or maybe the widespread assertion that girls grew up quicker than boys was true; but Mashenka's reasoning seemed older than Ron's now, although he was two years older than his sister.

Alina's heart sank again: how was it that her boy was among strangers, in a foreign country? It was just inconceivable that all that was happening to them was real. What was real to her began to seem more appropriate to a novel—something heart-wrenching and dramatic, like "Without Family" by Hector Malo, over which Alina had shed many tears as a child in her mother's cozy chair, the safest place in the world.

Chapter Eight

TOWARDS THE END OF the week, Oksana unexpectedly expressed a desire to go to Romania with Alina. Until then, during their joint walks in the city, which Oksana dubbed "nostalgic reveries of penetrating damp," she had consistently talked about returning to Israel as soon as possible, because no matter how nice it was to see her mother and sister, she had a duty to her daughters and husband.

Then there was her lover, David. Because although David had been the initiator in their relationship—and having fallen in love, he had, as he put it, thrown the whole world at her feet—Oksana still had to carry out the daily work of coddling their flame of love. She understood that even the strongest of flames was not immune to cooling after many years of coexistence. She had drawn a lucky card, having had no experience communicating with men—except for her unsuccessful but perhaps, therefore, still solid marriage—and Oksana didn't expect another chance. So, she cherished what she had, and all her thoughts and actions were directed only at that love. Therefore, the decision of her friend seemed, to Alina, completely unexpected and strange.

"I'll get a ticket for myself and Davidik," said Oksana, "to the ski resort in Poiana Brasov, as we've long needed a rest. Yes, and with you," she added turning to Alina, "we'll have company. It's not safe for a woman to go to Romania—this is not the most peaceful place, especially with two children—and Jonathan needs to go to his mother. And you can also get a ticket that allows you to spend a week with us and relax. Nothing in Greece will change that quickly."

Always when Oksana took the initiative and decided who should do what, it was a sure sign that her plans were well thought out. So, Alina didn't pester her friend with questions, knowing Oksana would tell her eventually. When their things were packed, and the children put to bed, and Katya and Dzhabril went to the cinema, Alina and Oksana were left alone to clear the remnants of a farewell dinner from the table. Oksana couldn't keep quiet any longer. "I actually didn't want to entangle you in this situation, but now that we are going together, I should tell you. Remember that friend I told you about who was in charge of a jewelry store? She asked me to do her a favor—to fly to Romania and meet with someone there who will change the stones in my earrings for diamonds. Since gold earrings will be included in my declaration when I enter Romania, there is no danger. Nobody will check what stones are in them. Agreed?"

"Sure, at first glance it seems quite simple and harmless. But you realize that these diamonds must be stolen! And if anyone is watching you, you'll be caught at the airport, or God forbid, during the exchange. Why doesn't your acquaintance go herself, if this is so safe?"

"She is connected with a jewelry store, and therefore knows about diamonds. But I know nothing. So even if they catch me, I can claim that I was unaware."

"Yes, you can say you changed your earrings at a spa, after a shower, and put on the wrong pair... I always felt you were an adventurer at heart, but not to this extent! You used to read detective stories from morning till night, so you must know what can happen.

"I'm not saying they will shoot you or put you in an electric chair, but even one year in a Romanian or, God forbid, Ukrainian prison can destroy a stronger person than you ... and how much will she pay you for this?"

"In what sense?" Oksana replied not understanding. "She's already paying for the ticket and the resort…"

"Ah, what nobility! So you get paid to go to jail? Sounds decent, and the money to care for your elderly mother and your children, while you rot in prison?" Alina countered, not seriously angry at her friend.

"Skip the black humor," Oksana grimaced. "She offered me twenty or twenty-five thousand dollars, but you see, she and her husband have helped my parents and sister a lot these past years."

"For free?" Alina couldn't resist.

"No, not for free, of course, but you know how it is in Ukraine. It's impossible to find anyone trustworthy, what with the crooks and extortionists. Anyone else would have taken the money and 'see ya.'"

Alina was helplessly silent. She knew her friend was stubborn. If Oksana had decided to do something, then no persuasion or exhortations would help. Oksana would remain silent or avert her eyes if prodded, but she would do what she wanted in the end. It was basically easier for her to go to jail than to refuse to help someone to whom she felt indebted. The amount that Oksana had been offered for "smuggling" was even more alarming, as it was a lot of money even on an international scale, never mind in Ukraine.

The doorbell interrupted a prolonged silence. Katya and Dzhabril had unexpectedly returned. It turned out that, on the way to the cinema, they had heard on the radio that an accident had occurred in a chemical plant, and all doctors, as well as those with experience in treating the wounded, were urged to help, since there weren't enough EMTs in the city.

Katya had completed some Red Cross classes, and immediately wanted to respond. Dzhabril, who was now working as a Red Cross doctor, of course was going to go with her. Alina went with him into the hallway, while Katya hastily changed her clothes in her bedroom.

"I'm leaving tomorrow, but we have not managed to talk during all this time. I owe you a lot…"

"You don't owe me anything. If not for you, I would never have come here. And I certainly wouldn't have met Katya. Every cloud has a silver lining." Dzhabril couldn't resist the urge to add, "I know what you're thinking—Katya or Alona, doesn't matter as long as it's a white woman. It's not like that at all! Alona was my youth, Kyiv, the university, the life of a wealthy foreigner. And Katya … you know, she looks like my mother."

Alina remembered the robed Arab woman with the dark worn hands. Dzhabril was silent for a while, perhaps trying to more accurately form his thoughts in Russian. His lean face was a bit smoother, because of the Ukrainian borsch and pies that Katya had regaled him with, and his skin had brightened somewhat, having been given a rest from the fierce Mediterranean sun. Since Dzhabril had arrived almost without any belongings, Katya had dressed him in Soviet-made shirts with long 70s-styled lapels, which she had bought once as part of her clothing "reserves," something all Ukrainians were familiar with. In these shirts, a tanned Dzhabril looked like a man from a remote farm, who had arrived in the city to look for a job.

"Yes," he continued, "Katya took pity on me. And the fact that she is also a beauty, what luck…"

Alina wanted to make a crack about what was more important in a woman, her soul or her appearance, but it was not the time to start such a discussion. "So you will remain in Ukraine, as you intended. What will you live on?"

"You can see, I have already started working for the Red Cross. I was promised a few days per week as an EMT. And, if we get married, perhaps I could work for the Red Cross in some friendly Arab country."

"I don't know how you managed this," Alina said surprised. "Here, local doctors with tons of experience have no jobs."

"But you know, you guys love foreigners," Dzhabril smiled slyly.

"I heard everything." Katya jumped out of the bedroom with a first aid bag at the ready. "And by the way, I haven't consented yet, and you're talking like we're already married." Grabbing Dzhabril by the hand, she pulled him out the door, not even saying farewell to Alina.

Well and for the best, thought Alina, who was not superstitious, but noting that Katya had not said goodbye when she should have, immediately rushed to finish the conversation.

In the morning, Alina and Oksana hardly said a word in the pre-departure bustle. When they got to the airport, however, their flight to Bucharest was delayed for three hours due to bad weather. They walked into a small waiting room, reminiscent of railway stations of years past—crowded, noisy and dirty. The children were rambunctious, and passengers sat and lay on benches, trunks, and even on the floor, making it impossible to take a step without stepping on someone. So where could one talk?

The friends sat side by side on a huge old suitcase of some stiff leathery material, like thick cardboard, which Oksana's grandmother had brought from Russia to richer Ukraine when she had gone seeking a better life. Davidik and Mashenka finally fell asleep on a bench which the adults had taken by force, and Jonathan wandered around their makeshift camp refusing to sit down for a second, as if he knew he was going home, although it was impossible to know what the boy understood from what he heard.

Alina tried several times to start a conversation with Oksana, who was dispassionately solving a crossword puzzle in a newspaper, but as soon as her eyes fell on the earrings with their huge transparent stones stretching across her friend's ears, her desire to communicate with the stubborn adventurer dissipated. Frustrated, Alina decided to pretend to be asleep, and put her head on her knees until she actually fell asleep. Then Oksana nudged her as the plane arrived.

Both were stubbornly silent on the plane, despite the fact that Alina had come to terms with Oksana's decision, and simply wanted to moan about her life—about her husband, whom she felt a keen jealousy over, knowing he was a man on his own, and yet felt equally, madly afraid for; about little Ron, who she had predicted herself, on an astrological chart, would have an unusual future; about her older boys, who, like Oksana's girls, were now in Israel in the army, which was the same as being on a barrel full of gunpowder, and there was no news from them. All week the friends had had practically no time to have a heart to heart: every minute someone had demanded their attention—children, Oksana's mother, Katya, Dzhabril or Marina. Alina had been counting on these couple of hours on the plane.

Chapter Nine

THE ARRIVAL OF ALINA and Oksana in Bucharest was marked by a warm downpour. The rain melted yesterday's snow which still lay in a dense layer, as if it could flood the ice that had formed between the two friends. Groups of young workers in orange overalls propped themselves up against the walls of the hangars that littered the airfield. They smoked, spat, and trampled cigarette butts into islands of pure snow preserved between the metal beams. Not working, and supposedly hiding from the rain, the young robust guys entertained themselves by making fun of the passengers who were scurrying to the bus, sludging snow into their shoes or boots. Cuddling the children, Alina and Oksana, soaked to the skin, didn't hesitate to exchange views on the legacy of socialism, which left indelible marks on society, such as these workers.

The airport, which subtly resembled Ternopil, was also a shard of the crash of socialism. Even in Kyiv, Alina had been struck by the wretchedness of such structures made of glass and concrete, which had been touted as the peak of modern architecture.

The chicest thing to do at one time was to take a party full of people and rush off to the airport. It was their "window to the world." What could be more exciting than sipping coffee with cognac at the counter of a 24-hour café, and reading the ever-changing electronic displays of arrival and departure schedules, as if they were a form of modern poetry?

Later, after Alina left Ukraine, she had never again been so fascinated by flight schedules. Paris to London, New York to

72

Miami, were nothing compared to Kyiv to Yerevan, or Kyiv to Vladivostok. Such was the desire to see the world back then, to be in a new place, to try on a different life. Did this desire really fade with age…? Alina didn't remember when she had last wanted something so passionately, with such excitement. I wish I could bring my loved ones together, she thought, so that everything could be as before… And then she remembered the famous Soviet anthem for tourism, "I don't need the Turkish coast, and I don't need Africa."

It was surprisingly fast to get a taxi, since they were queued, but the road from Bucharest to Brashev took four hours over dull terrain, where one miserable village viewed from the window of the cab smoothly merged into another. In one village though, the snow on the roofs of the miserable huts turned the shacks into a beautiful New Year's scene. In the mountains which marked the entrance to Brashev, the landscape changed a little, but it was here on the deserted mountain passes that Alina became more alarmed, as she recalled all sorts of terrible stories about rapists and murderers.

From the back of the cab, it was as if Alina could feel danger emanating from their gloomy driver through his very skin. He was silent all the way, the only sound coming from the creaks of his new leather jacket, as he rubbed the red shaved nape of his neck with his palm. He reminded Alina of the Bratva from films about the Russian mafia. She was afraid to say even a word to Oksana. What if the driver understood Russian or Hebrew?

Brashev, as befits a ski resort, was covered in snow. Upon arrival, Alina and Oksana wondered what to do first—find a boarding house or bring Jonathan to his mother? They hadn't contacted her earlier because there was no telephone service between Ternopil and Brashev.

As it turned out, the dilemma was resolved by Jonathan, who recognized the main street along which they drove, or, better said, the huge Christmas tree in the square. It was here that the previous year Jonathan had seen Santa with his mom and dad, and had received a real computer in such a huge box that Santa Claus himself had to load it into the trunk of the car, as the boy's father was too elderly to lift it. And so it was opposite this Christmas tree that the boy now burst into tears and, for the first time in so many weeks, began to ask for his mother—just like Mashenka had.

"The child is right," the taxi driver suddenly declared in such simple and understandable English that even Alina understood him. The driver had apparently understood Jonathan through the chaotic mixture of Romanian and Hebrew. "Your street is nearby, in the section of new villas. I know this boy's family. His father is a millionaire from Israel."

Alina really didn't like this unexpected remark and was even more suspicious of the driver. Hearing that they were almost there, she breathed a sigh of relief, grateful that the unpleasant journey would soon end.

Having unloaded the suitcases, the driver looked at Oksana through veiled eyes, and said in English something like, "I won't say goodbye." Alina told herself that she must have misunderstood the phrase, since her knowledge of English left much to be desired, unlike Oksana who had studied English as a child, and went on to major in English at an institute for foreign languages. However, Oksana let the incident go without a comment.

The meeting of Jonathan and his mother followed almost the same scenario as the meeting of Alina with her daughter. At the sound of the doorbell, a beautiful full woman of about fifty with the sad face of an older Madonna opened the door. The boy rushed to his mother in tears, and she, weakened by the joy she felt, fell upon him, clinging to him tightly, and whispered something soothing and affectionate in Romanian to him, completely forgetting the presence of anyone else.

Alina and Oksana, standing on the threshold with their prehistoric suitcases, also sniffled, and the sleepy and exhausted Davidik and Mashenka cried because everyone else was crying.

This touching scene was watched from the next room, through an open door, by a young man with piercing black almond-shaped eyes and a musketeer's mustache. He did not get up from his computer to approach their charming little group. Blinking away tears, Alina made out a wheelchair and saw that his knees were covered with a plaid cloth.

An hour later, after having fed the children and put them to bed, the adults, having been introduced and now knowing who was who, had dinner at a table in the clean, bright kitchen. Oksana and Jacques, the man in the wheelchair who turned out to be the son of the woman, conducted a posh conversation in English. Jacques offered to show Oksana a new game of solitaire on his computer. Although it would have been wrong to refuse, she readily accepted because in actuality she loved all kinds of games.

Alina, half listening, watched the movements of the mistress of the house, and sensed that she was somehow now enveloped in an unusual sensation of complete serenity. It seemed that time had stopped and there was no war, no separation, no fear, no endless road; there was only this cozy house, a Christmas tree, a caring mother and the children sleeping on the other side of the wall.

Sofia, which was the name of Jonathan's mother, gently stirred the tea in the teapot. She reminded Alina of a friend from her youth, whom she had loved to visit. It felt just as calm now as it had been then, sitting in a kitchen, remarking at her hostess's command of the stove, learning culinary tips mixed with heartfelt stories. In her friend's eyes, Alina had been young and stupid. Although she had been married for ten years and had two children, she had "so much to learn." In that kitchen, Alina could reveal anything without fear of being condemned or betrayed.

And now Alina broke down. Like twenty years ago, she started talking and could not stop. Alina didn't hear Jacques and Oksana loudly discussing a solitaire move, and then quieting down behind the door as they heard her confused revelations; or the clock striking an hour, and a child waking, only to fall asleep again a moment later. Alina just talked…

Sofia, who understood Russian well enough, but could only speak a few simple phrases, sat with her hand on her cheek, occasionally inserting one or two words in Romanian. Alina sat opposite her, begging to be heard. The tea cooled in cups made of German porcelain, as the voices behind the wall fell silent. The clock struck two as Alina, having finished her childhood and adolescence, having dealt with her first marriage and her cheating husband, had already moved on to the difficulties of emigration and to meeting Him, the love of her life.

She talked about her crazy love, about how she almost lost him; that having destroyed her family, she went to her beloved with two suitcases and two children; about how she bore him two more; and how this damn war had scattered them all over the world.

It wasn't that Sofia's fate seemed easier. After all, the woman had agreed to become a surrogate mother for a 70-year-old because she needed the money to cure her disabled son. But there was such kindness in the simple woman, as if she had enough kindness for all the afflicted and tired, while she herself remained strong.

That night, no one went to bed, and in the morning, peppy despite a lack of sleep, the friends gathered their things, as Oksana needed to go to the ski house, and Alina to the ticket office to get plane tickets to Athens. They drank their morning coffee to the Romanian news, with interruptions for advertisements for toothpaste and Mercedes. Oksana laughed at some jokes of Jacques's, then suddenly, raising her eyes to the screen, cried out in surprise, "Look, look!" She shook Alina's shoulder. "That's Ira! The woman with the gold!"

On the screen, a slender woman in handcuffs walked with her head bowed in the escort of Ukrainian police. Alina shot Oksana a meaningful look. Jacques, who usually did not take his eyes off Oksana, realized that she was somewhat excited by this news story, and translated into plain English that the

Romanian and Ukrainian security services had uncovered a criminal gang engaged in smuggling jewelry. In fact, the criminals had exported Ceausescu's diamond collection in dribs and drabs, and the diamonds had disappeared without a trace within a year of the dictator's execution, but now they were found, and it was discovered that they had been smuggled out by one of his former ministers.

"That woman," Jacques explained, pointing to the ill-fated Ira, "was the smuggler's link. She received jewelry from Romania and sent it to Odessa, where they were sold for huge amounts to nouveau rich Russians."

Oksana sat white as chalk… Alina cursed herself for allowing her friend to get involved in this mess, at the same time realizing that she could not change what had already happened. Without exchanging a word or a look, they both knew that plans would have to be changed. Alina pulled Oksana into the corridor (away from Jacques' prying ears) and resolutely declared that they should fly to Greece all together, and that she was on her way to buy tickets for everyone. Oksana had better be waiting for her, and not even step out onto the street.

At the travel agency, Alina was shocked by the news that all Bucharest to Athens flights were canceled for a week because of the Turkish-Greek conflict, which had spread from the distant islands to the capital. Turkish warships now stood off the Greek coast forming another hotbed of tension in the world.

For Alina, this cruelly meant the following: she couldn't get to Israel or Greece now. She would have to wait for the resumption of flights, tormented by thoughts of her son, but there was no other way… A trip in a roundabout way, for example, via Italy, and then by sea, would take no less time. And there was no money for it anyway. Alina's husband, on the day of her unexpected visit, had only been able to get a thousand dollars, which had been enough to get to Ukraine. The dollars and gold, which Alina had entrusted to Oksana in Israel, and Oksana had returned to her, had to be saved for Greece, for who knew how long they would have to stay there…

Chapter Ten

RETURNING HOME WITH BAD news, which could even become fatal for Oksana, Alina couldn't sit down. But Sofia wouldn't allow her friends to succumb to despondency. She outlined a plan, which Jacques translated from Romanian. Everything would turn out fine. Sofia would take Alina with all the children to her son Michal, who lived not far away at their hotel in Poiana-Brashev. Sofia and Jacques traditionally went there for the New Year. Vlad, her eldest son, the most capable and least settled, should also be arriving from Germany. He was currently working part-time in Frankfurt as a laborer, despite the fact that he had a law degree which meant that he knew the innards of Romanian legality firsthand. In fact, he had left for Western Europe in the hope of continuing his education there.

Oksana would stay in Brashev. Jacques would keep her company, and the hotel would just have to do without a computer geek right now, especially since he also had a lot of urgent work at home. Jacques did not specify why Oksana should stay, but it seemed to Alina that he had plans of his own—and was ever hopeful—the shine in his eyes betraying the young man.

Jacques had not been disabled from birth—he had been injured in a car accident and considered his condition to be temporary. To get back on his feet, he had to undergo several more operations, but Jacques seemed to take it in stride and looked to the future with optimism, especially when Oksana's warm blue eyes rested on him with apparently genuine sympathy. Alina really didn't want to leave Oksana alone with this guy, but they were staying here, so Alina did not object to the owners' proposal.

As for celebrating the New Year, she and Oksana had not planned to celebrate it together. Over the years of living as immigrants, this once most beloved holiday had faded and been forgotten, because it was not officially celebrated in Israel. There was no snow. The pre-New Year excitement, when all the stores were full of Christmas tree decorations, was simply missing. There were no decorated Christmas trees, no lights in the streets, no festivities. Seemingly imperceptibly, the New Year moved to September, with the meager dipping of sliced apples in honey replacing the clink of champagne glasses.

But having arrived in Poiana-Brashev, Alina and the children immediately plunged into the New Year's bustle. The hotel served mainly Israeli tourists, so a tree was not usually placed in the lobby. But this year, some of the rooms were occupied by Russian and German tour groups, who did not want to give up their holiday for the sake of Jewish "whims." The management of the hotel, that is, Michal, had had to compromise and, preparing the restaurant hall for a festive dinner, put small Christmas trees on the tables for the Germans and Russians.

It cannot be said that the decoration of the hall or the dinner itself were strikingly luxurious. There was no extra money, and Michal, as a manager, had to squeeze the most out of every leu in order to somehow create a festive atmosphere for his guests and family. Unfortunately, Vlad could not come. Yoram, Sofia's husband and Jonathan's father, was stuck in Israel and could not help, although he was the owner of the hotel. The family had not received any news from Yoram for a long time, except for the message brought by Alina that he had enrolled in the civil defense detachment.

Sofia spoke of her husband, if not with tenderness, then with great respect. And she raised her son Jonathan to be reverent of his father. It was for his sake that this far-fetched enterprise had been started: to "sire" a child at seventy years old, and even pay her to bear it. Alina remembered Yoram's noble face and his absolutely incredible proposal. If only Sofia knew that it was Alina that Yoram had first chosen to be Jonathan's surrogate mother, when he had originally planned to raise the child in Israel! How bizarrely human destinies sometimes intersected…

But if Alina had married Yoram, tempted as she was by his money, then not only would Sofia have been ultimately unhappy, but Alina herself would have been bound by inseparable ties (Yoram's condition was that they would never divorce) into an unnatural marriage. If she had taken upon herself the responsibility of raising someone else's child, she would not have been able to return to her beloved, and then neither Ron nor Mashenka would have been born…

A loud noise interrupted Alina's thoughts, and she peered out of the room where Michal had put her, together with Sofia and the children, as if they were all one family. This room, recently a billiard room, was next to the manager's office, and having now opened the door, Alina found herself in the thick of things.

Several disheveled women, whom Alina easily recognized as her compatriots, rushed into Michal's office, bellowing indignantly in Hebrew, its characteristic scandalous intonation readily familiar to Alina.

Michal, stocky, unhurried, his face pitted with smallpox, had a red mustache and blue, slightly narrowed eyes. Outwardly he was the complete opposite of his younger brother. Having received no form of higher education, he had made a good career in these troubled times by opening a business transporting food and souvenirs from Germany. In Germany, he had bought a small truck for the business and didn't skimp on a garage and anti-theft devices.

When Yoram decided to go into the hotel business in Romania, and acquired the building of an empty government sanatorium—once one of the most prestigious resorts in Romania, ornamented by columns, arches, and marble statues—no one had any doubts that it was Michal, with his business savvy and entrepreneurial spirit, who would become its manager.

Now he was dealing with the most unpleasant part of his official duties—working with disgruntled clients, and namely, repelling their attacks. Although Michal had learned to speak a little Hebrew, he could not get a word in edgewise. Even Alina could not immediately understand what exactly these indignant women wanted. Some were too cold, and they demanded that the heat be turned on, others too hot, demanding the heat be turned off.

Someone's bed creaked, the mattresses were too hard, somewhere in the bathroom a light went out... Their complaints poured in, in a continuous stream, a tangle of hysteria, confusion, and contradictions. The simple answer was that these people were tired. The Israelis, mostly women with children, were not tourists here, but refugees, hostages of the war. They had nowhere to go, and many were already in debt to the owner, as Sofia had lamented yesterday, yet they couldn't be driven out into the street.

"The hotel is suffering losses! Pay first, then demand!" Alina shouted, rushing to the rescue of Michal, convinced that there was no other way to resist this onslaught.

Over the fifteen years of her life in Israel, she had learned to speak the language of the "natives," that is to say, to respond with a shout to a scream if necessary, but, having been brought up on Tolstoy and Chekhov, she still felt uneasy doing so. Alina knew that her own scream would reverberate in her ears for a long time, making her frown, as if from a toothache, with shame.

Especially now, when there were women in front of her, worried about the fate of their husbands, sons, and parents; tired of the cold, the lack of money and the uncertainty of this "indefinite exile" in a foreign land. But, knowing from life's experiences that true justice does not exist, Alina, caught between the equally justified Michal and the exhausted refugees, chose the one to whom she owed more, due to her circumstances, and frankly her personal sympathy.

Michal was really personable. He was one of those men who personified confidence and reliability, and everyone who met him, especially women, were drawn to this calm haven. He was not a womanizer, did not cast lustful glances at women, and actually acted indifferently to everything except business and his family.

His family consisted of his wife and his elderly grandmother, who was settled here under the pretext that she would be able to receive treatment at the resort. In reality she was at the resort because Sofia, who usually got along well with people, could not get along with her ex-mother-in-law. She had not managed to forgive the old woman for her hostile attitude when Sofia, a girl from the provinces, had first come to visit her classmate, who would become her husband; for the woman's conspicuous absence from their wedding; for her reluctance to look after their children during the summer holidays; and for her indifference to the fate of her youngest grandson when she had refused to provide for the operation for Jacques, claiming that it wouldn't help anyway.

This last offense was the most painful, because the refusal of her mother-in-law had served, from Sofia's point of view, as the indirect cause of death of her first husband, who, hoping to earn the necessary funds, had gone to work in Israel and had died under unexplained circumstances, allegedly at work. Who knew what had happened to him in that distant hot country? Maybe he overstrained himself doing backbreaking physical labor to which he was not accustomed. Either way, the widow did not receive a penny of insurance, if he had any, and even the money that her husband had managed to earn went, according to the employer, to ferry the body of the deceased home. The day of her husband's funeral, Sofia stopped talking to his mother.

Now the old woman, wiry and with a back straight as a retired ballerina's, performed the role of doorman in the hotel and told everyone that this was her "swan song."

Michal's wife, thin, and with the appearance of a Romani which was so common in Romania, was the complete opposite of him. She rushed through the corridors of the hotel like a whirlwind, changing direction depending on whether it was necessary to shout an order to the bellboy or the maid. The spouses complemented each other perfectly as they managed the family business. And the fact that they were childless, which was due to an illness the wife had suffered (Jacques had shared several family secrets with Oksana), did not seem to prevent them from living in perfect harmony.

The first days of the new year were marked by heavy snowfall. It was impossible to leave the yard, and skiing was canceled. Alina sculpted a family of snowmen with her children—not a selfless act since she yearned for the snow. The "family" was lined up along the path leading to the main entrance.

There was dad with glasses made of wire, and Ron with blue button eyes, and even Jacques with a musketeer mustache, for whom Jonathan donated a watercolor brush. (The boy was very fond of drawing, and had a promising career as an artist.) Then, in the yard, two long areas were trod upon and filled with water to make two long paths of ice. They ran down them, accelerating furiously, the goal being to make it to the end without falling, which took almost aerobatic skill.

They didn't get to ski the big slopes for the entire week, as the lifts were closed due to heavy snowfall. But neither Alina nor the children were particularly upset. They weren't avid athletes, and how much did a person need to properly experience winter? You could make a snowball in your bare hand, or veer sideways on a sled, as you dashed around a soft snowdrift...

So Alina, devoting her days to winter fun, and her evenings to helping Michal's wife and mother set the tables for dinner and wash the dishes in the kitchen—in order to save money, the waiters and kitchen staff had been sent home for the winter holidays—brought herself daily to the brink of exhaustion and, reaching her bed, slept not only without nightmares, but without dreams until dawn.

But when Michal, having finally connected with the airport, told Alina that the first flight from Bucharest to Athens was scheduled for the next day, she and Davidik and Mashenka got into a taxi within the hour. Sofia would also return home with them. When they said goodbye to Michal and his family on the columned hotel porch, Alina had a lump in her throat, as Michal had truly made her feel like family for her brief stay.

"Oksana!" Alina shouted from the doorway, as soon as she and Sofia returned to Brashev, "Get ready quickly! We're going to the airport. The flight is tomorrow!"

"Why go today if the flight is tomorrow?" Oksana was confused.

"Do you think we're the only ones who want to fly away? There have been no flights for a week. We will be the first."

Alina, who had absorbed the Soviet habit of queuing all night with her mother's milk, as they say, was not going to jeopardize the situation.

Oksana hesitated. "Maybe you should go to the airport without me. You stand in line and buy tickets, and David and I will arrive in the morning. I know that this is disgusting—to send you there all night—but you have to understand: I cannot leave Jacques like this, all of a sudden." Oksana nodded towards the closed door.

This, Alina could understand. She knew she would be bored out of her mind at the airport, but she would go alone by bus, and let Oksana figure out her own plan... Alina thought to leave Mashenka with Oksana, but then decided that she wouldn't take the risk. She vowed she would never part with her children again, because who knew what might happen?

Oksana did arrive in the morning, as she had promised, but with someone else in tow. David was there as expected, but Jacques was also there in his wheelchair. They moved purposefully through the crowd that parted in front of them. From the onset they made a strong impression: a slender red-haired woman with blue eyes, and a handsome "musketeer" in a wheelchair.

Jacques' confident look and sparkling eyes left no doubt that this condition was temporary for him. And such an aura hovered over this couple that when the procession reached her Alina did not begin, as she had wanted to, to tell her tale about the tickets. Alina had stood in line for the tickets only to discover that she could only buy three tickets, as they had run out of seats. But she had managed to snatch a ticket from a military man, who, having unexpectedly received a message that his vacation was extended for a week, was in such a hurry to get back to his wife that he was going to just throw away the ticket. It had taken quite a bit of persuasion on her part to get him to agree to go to the cashier and re-register the ticket in her name. "Let it go," she thought.

Alina looked at Oksana, on whose ears another pair of earrings were hanging today—not the ones with transparent stones that she had smuggled out. These were a bit Romani-looking as they were massive gold rings. Alina caught Jacques' eyes—of course, his gift. "She's not going," thought Alina and, like an echo, she heard:

"I'm not going to Greece. Sorry… Hand over our tickets."

"Why do you have suitcases then?" Alina did not understand.

"I, or rather, we are going to Germany, to Vlad. It is impossible to return to Israel now. In Ukraine I am now a persona non grata, and here, in Romania, I can be arrested at any moment."

"And what do I say to your husband, your girls?" Alina could not ask about David. She could not speak freely at all. Jacques was piercing her with his black eyes, and probably understood at least a little Russian. "So," Alina quickly added, "you will go with me to the toilet, to help me with Mashenka, and Davidik will wait with Jacques."

She practically dragged Oksana along, trying not to slip on the grated linoleum of the airport. Mashenka could hardly keep up with them.

"Can you explain to me what's going on?" Alina's left eye began to twitch a little from overexcitement.

"I thought you understood," Oksana answered softly, then continued in a stronger tone. "I love him and will be with him as long as he desires me. Don't look at me like that: I know that he is disabled, but that's temporary! He has two operations left to go, and we will soon have money for the first one." Oksana's hand mechanically reached for the earrings.

Alina gasped, "You did it after all! How? When?"

Oksana was silent.

"But you said that you did not need the money," Alina could not resist sneering.

"Now it's needed, very much needed," Oksana stubbornly answered, refusing to acknowledge the put down.

"But how do you plan to get any money? Your friend, as you saw, is in prison."

"You haven't been to Ukraine in a long time," Oksana was already turning to leave the restroom, nervously fingering her bag. "This friend got out the next day and is safely in Germany."

"And David? What should I tell him?" Alina imagined the face of the small, self-satisfied—despite his balding crown and protruding tummy—Iraqi Jew distorted into the grimace of a crying clown—a face she found completely impossible to endure. Large tears rolled down the cheeks of the man who was so easily given to crying.

"He is not the kind of person to stay alone for very long."

"But you and David didn't have a fling. You've been together for years. And love? You loved him…"

"A protracted romance is exactly what kills love!" Oksana said with conviction. "I don't know whether I loved David or only accepted love. Now it seems to me that I'm really in love for the first time."

"Mother! Mother! They called our plane!" shouted Davidik, popping open the door of the ladies' room.

The friends almost ran back to Jacques, unable any longer to explore the burning female question of love.

Oksana's plane left an hour earlier than Alina's, again leaving Alina alone. And during this hour, as Mashenka dozed next to her on a hard bench in the waiting room, Alina thought about the vicissitudes of love… What had happened to David and Oksana had awakened long-standing fears in her.

The one who tries to conquer the person whom he loves, invests all of himself—and he sometimes wins. But time passes, and the conquered one suddenly wakes up after a long sleep no longer wanting to be a prisoner in a golden cage, but wanting to be a creator of love herself—to work, to suffer, to doubt… After all, only what is obtained at the cost of great effort is truly appreciated.

So what would happen when her beloved woke up from the magical dream that Alina had enveloped him in, when he wanted to escape from the golden cage of her embrace? What would happen to her then?

Chapter Eleven

ODDLY ENOUGH, IT WAS snowing in Greece when Alina and Mashenka arrived. They thought they had bid snow farewell in Romania. It was a shame that they were not in Jerusalem to see that snow had also fallen there. Yet here, in Athens, as she later learned from a guard at the parliament building, the temperature had dropped so low that the guardsmen, who were dressed in their traditional folk uniforms were given a piquant addition—warm pants. There had not been such a cold winter for six years, in Europe, or America, or in the Mediterranean. Nature seemed to be deliberately responding cataclysmically to the madness of humankind.

Alina was so pensive waiting for the luggage that she didn't notice when Mashenka climbed onto the conveyor belt, where suitcases and bags were beginning to joyfully jump as they were pulled from the aircraft. Running up, Alina raked her daughter off the assembly line of bags, along with a military-style canvas bag which she had bought in Bucharest at a flea market. Her heirloom antique suitcase had been taken by Oksana to Germany.

Alina only had a few things, which was enough: two Soviet-made children's flannel suits from Katya's stock, and two hand-knitted sweaters that Sofia had made for Alina's children from wool she obtained in the village. In Brashev, the market was crammed with similar homemade products, but the Romanians themselves didn't wear these sweaters, preferring imported ones—mostly from Turkey—which reminded Alina of

Ukraine. However, Alina preferred unpretentious hand-knitted items, and Sofia's gift now came in very useful.

One sweater she pulled over Masha, who from time to time shrugged her shoulders, trying to get rid of the prickly sting from the homespun wool, while yet rejoicing in the warmth. The second sweater was ready for Ron.

Alina had rehearsed the scene countless times while waiting at the airport, and during her flight. She saw before her a glowing neon sign: "Divan Palace." She imagined herself entering the hotel and asking the receptionist, in English—she had rehearsed this small speech with Oksana many times—what Louise's room number was.

"Divan Palace," the cute young taxi driver with an earring broadened his sweet smile in expectation of a tip. Having received an astronomical amount of drachmas at the airport exchange, she almost paid him too little, as her mind scrambled to figure out how many zeros to add for the correct payment. Then, barely restraining her impatience, she dragged Mashenka to the receptionist.

To her clearly articulated request, which followed all the rules of English grammar, as to which room Louise Amelek was staying in, the response was very clear: there was no such surname on the guest list. Alina couldn't believe it. So the young, plump Greek woman with a pug nose—not at all the classic profile of statues—turned the screen monitor towards Alina, and tried to find the rather simple surname various ways by changing the spelling several times. Yet she was not successful.

The girl triumphantly turned away, with the aplomb of youth that knows no compassion, and Alina, bewildered, sank into a leather chair in the luxurious lobby. There was only one hotel with this name in the city. Alina had checked at the airport information desk. Almost immediately, a young waiter in a snow-white waistcoat leapt to her side, offering something to drink. Alina, bewildered, nodded her head gratefully. However, upon remembering the state of her finances, she decided to only order cocoa and cream for Mashenka.

For such a turn of events Alina was completely unprepared. She had been sure that in the weeks following the arrival of the refugee ship to the free shores of Greece, Louise, with her children and Ron, would have chosen to remain at this hotel. Alina looked up at the huge crystal chandelier and garlands of fresh flowers hanging from the ceiling. It became obvious now that this was an insanely expensive hotel.

Preparing to make a second trip to the receptionist to inquire whether any Christians from Israel were staying at all, and who had booked their rooms, Alina, brows knit in concentration, tried to remember the random English words from her schoolbooks which she now needed.

Mashenka meanwhile was at war with her hot cocoa because she was afraid to stain her old, but very dressy white coat. Oksana's daughters had once flaunted this coat, one after the other, and when the girls grew out of it, the valuable thing was faithfully packed away and hidden on a closet shelf, in the hopes that someday it would come in handy again. And so it did. Alina unbuttoned Mashenka's buttons and freed her from the fur coat, all the while repeating her English phrases over and over again, so as not to forget what she needed to say and how to say it properly.

She was unlucky that, as she was rehearsing, a new receptionist started her shift, and instead of an unfriendly but at least professional girl, an arrogant bleached blonde now appeared at the counter. This new girl refused to understand Alina until she switched to Russian out of despair.

It turned out that nouveau rich Russians were respected in Greece—and not because Greeks read the novels of Leo Tolstoy. The "New Russians," with their uncontrolled spending, had firmly paved their way into the hearts of the peasant-like, thrifty and tight-lipped Greeks.

An elderly Russian maid of Greek descent, who had emigrated ten years earlier from Mariupol, was brought in from somewhere. She had a high lacquered hairdo, as if she still styled her hair at a Soviet barbershop. She told Alina that a large group of Christian Arabs had indeed stayed there one night in December, and the police had even set up several posts in the square in front of the hotel, as they were concerned about potential Muslim terrorists. But the rooms had not been reserved by representatives of the Greek Orthodox Church, but by an attaché of the Lebanese embassy.

This hit Alina hard. She would not be allowed in the Lebanese embassy.

"Does Madam want to stay at our hotel until she solves her problems?"

"No, madam does not want to." Alina was already dressing Mashenka. Madam wanted the cheapest hotel in town…

"Very cheap," she explained to the taxi driver.

Trying not to think about what to do next, or how to get into the Lebanese embassy, Alina distracted herself with the thought that Russian was truly becoming an international language: how many times during these past days had it been Russians who had helped her out?

"We're here. You can get out."

The driver, this time elderly and mustachioed, with a ridiculous surname, Ivanopoulos, also turned out to be a Russian emigrant, who was quite successful by local standards. Greek city taxis, painted in the same muddy yellow, and scratched and dirty, seemed miserable compared to Israeli Mercedes, but for the locals, and even more so for the immigrants, being a taxi driver meant stable support for themselves and their families.

Alina, who wasn't yet accustomed to not having adequate funds, did not skimp on his tip. Her money was melting away like snow, and she suddenly became keenly interested in how people earned a living. Alina knew what hard times were—she herself was an emigrant, and her business, which she had had to close after the birth of her children, had taught her to count her pennies. However, six years of a fairly prosperous life with her husband, during which time the bank never threatened to close her accounts and she didn't need to save on trifles, had helped her to forget the lessons of emigration—the lessons of survival.

The shabby appearance of the hotel at which the former compatriot had dropped them off brought back memories of her emigration, when she and her first husband had rented their first apartment in a similar area of Haifa.

The entrance to the hotel "lobby" was right on the roadway of one of the central arteries of the industrial region of Athens. This area was replete with wholesale warehouses, tumultuous dirt, crowds of people at bus stops, smog and stench, and gray snow from the emissions of a factory that spouted a smell of burnt rubber throughout the entire district. Against this background, the pretentious "Hotel" sign on the peeling wall looked like a ridiculous joke.

The innkeeper, lanky and casually dressed, with a drooping mustache and a puffy face, was also the manager, accountant and concierge. He spent whole days playing cards with the fat owner of a nearby café and two other suspicious types. A room without a door, which was ludicrously called the boss's office, was located directly at the entrance, so that from the street one could observe the small company imposingly located around a card table, while the proletariat toiled in a neighboring factory. However, the location of the room had a strategic message as well, since no one could enter or leave unnoticed.

Judging by the fact that the owner took the payment in advance and in cash, Alina concluded that anyone was welcome here. Therefore, when they were offered a choice of a room for four which had a toilet but would also be shared with two strangers, or a room for two which only had a sink, Alina chose the latter. The common "amenities" were located at the end of a gloomy, narrow corridor. It was a normal men's restroom with chipped urinals and three toilet stalls. Only the center booth was closed with a plywood door, which bore the gallant inscription: "For Ladies."

Entering the cramped room, Alina threw her bag on the bed, and sat Mashenka on it as well. She looked around to see that the walls were shabby, and the windows unwashed. However, the radiator under the window generated heat, the beds had clean linen, water flowed from the tap, and most importantly, for the first time in many days, they would sleep in their own room!

Alina tried to lock the door, but it was impossible to do so from the inside. She decided she'd have to move the bed there for the night, as there was nothing more suitable in the room. The interior was complemented by a board screwed to the wall, apparently intended to serve as a table, and two nails sticking out of the door, on which Alina solemnly hung her and Mashenka's outerwear.

The meager circumstances did not depress Alina at all. On the contrary, it was even fun. As always in difficult situations, the feelings of despair and fear which had previously filled her began to melt into a compressed spring full of inner strength. "Just survive!" pulsated in her temples.

Alina warmed some water in a glass pasta jar with an immersion water heater. She had stubbornly carried both with her from Ukraine. The interesting thing was that neither the Ukrainian nor Romanian customs officers had found fault with her. They recognized that these things were traditional necessities for those traveling abroad, as well as an opportunity to save money.

After washing and laying Mashenka down, Alina opened a guidebook in Russian, which she had bought at the airport with the expectation that she would show the children the Acropolis and the Temple of Dionysius, and take them to museums to acquaint them with Greek antiquities. For the same reason, her bag also contained Myths of Ancient Greece, which Katya had never returned to the library. Now her children's cultural education would have to be postponed, as the only thing that Alina was currently interested in was the address of the Lebanese embassy.

Sitting on the bed, Alina thoughtfully leafed through the thin pages. The Athens which she had first seen thirteen years ago, traveling with her first husband, was nothing like the tempting description in the travel guide. She had not seen the glorious capital of ancient Hellas with marble palaces and shady parks, where ancient heroes once lived and gods fell in love with earthly women, but a city where heroes, if they were lucky, turned the steering wheel of a taxi, and women in cheap pumps bought at a seasonal sale, and wearing threadbare suits, shivered in the morning chill at bus stops. They went to hotels, shops, restaurants serving tourists, and they got such pennies for their work that they didn't even bother to wipe the tables in the café, or brush the white dust of another excavation from the newsstand kiosk. And the gods … the gods were disassembled in museums and did not see what had happened to their fiefdom.

Alina's reflections were interrupted by the sound of footsteps in the corridor, and almost immediately someone pushed against the door. She praised herself for having thought to move the bed. It occurred to her to pretend to be asleep, but curiosity overcame her fear. In her soul, she felt a sudden hope that one of her own had found her, although no one could have known where she was.

Alina pushed the bed aside slightly and tried to look through a crack in the frame, but the strip of light created by the dim bulb in the corridor was partially obscured by a massive figure. Pulling the door open a little more, Alina practically buried her nose in the fat belly of the owner of the nearby café, who was trying to peer into the room.

Content that Alina was in the room, he bared his teeth in an oily smile and, rummaging in his pocket, pulled out a crumpled twenty-dollar bill.

Realizing what was going on, Alina at first was offended, but then she remembered that in Greece twenty dollars was decent money. So she grinned and shook her head. The night visitor, convinced that he had offered too little, hid the first bill and took out fifty dollars. Alina was no longer amused, and she tried to slam the door, but the fat man inserted his chubby leg—decked out in a narrow stylish boot with fancy buckles—into the gap and, with a theatrical sigh, added the previous twenty to the fifty-dollar bill.

"Go away! Leave now! I'll call the police! I have a child here!" Alina tried to reason with the uninvited guest in Russian, forgetting that Greece was not Romania, and Russian was not routinely studied here.

Resting her shoulder against the door, Alina reproached herself for the incident. Two hours earlier, while the owner had taken out the room key and leisurely counted her money, Alina had been staring too closely at this short man. With his bald head, black mustache, and smug look, he reminded her of David—now Oksana's former lover. David was an Iraqi Jew, and this one was a Greek or a Turk. The ethnic characteristics of appearance had always been of interest to Alina. However, she had completely forgotten the rule she had learned in her first year in Israel—do not look directly at a man, otherwise you will be misunderstood—and now she was paying for it with a sleepless night.

Angry, Alina pushed the bed back to the door with as much force as she could muster, and seemingly caught the leg of the unlucky gentleman, who, with a shrill yelp, hobbled away along the corridor, muttering curses under his breath. Alina sighed deeply, thanking God that Mashenka had not woken up.

The next day, Alina and her daughter went out at dawn. The hotel manager's room was empty, and Alina, determined to look for the Lebanese embassy, decided it was best to not even report the night incident. They finally found Kifissias Avenue at lunchtime, after several attempts to use a map from the guidebook. Having found it though, Alina felt no comfort, as she didn't dare to go near the doors of the embassy for fear of being noticed.

They took up an observation post in the café opposite and went through three cups of coffee (Alina black, and Mashenka with milk)—the cheapest drink on the menu. Alina gazed at the massive door, which a stern, guardsman-like doorman respectfully opened for mustachioed men in black, but she did not know how to get in there with her Israeli passport and rudimentary English.

They returned home in a crowded bus, hungry and disappointed. It was difficult for Alina to explain to Masha why it was impossible to enter the building that they had been looking for for hours, why it was unfeasible to ask the mustachioed uncles where Ron was now, or even show them Ron's photograph. The little girl too clearly remembered how last year when they were looking for her friend's lost puppy, they had gone to all the neighboring houses with the puppy's photograph, only to have the puppy eventually show up at her friend's house—drenched, shabby and guilty-looking.

The next morning, Alina and Mashenka went to the same café, hoping to take up their observation post again. The owner, slick, fat, and wearing a fez, stood on a stepladder, straightening the Turkish flags hanging from the ceiling above the cash register, but when he saw them entering, he was not too lazy to get down. An idler who was a regular at the café (Alina had seen him yesterday, unshaven and in the same stale shirt) obligingly held the door, while the owner pushed them out of the café with his belly, declaring there was no coffee. Either he mistook Alina for a terrorist, or he was just angry that they had sat all day, ordering only a few cups of coffee.

Stone-faced, Alina grabbed Mashenka into her arms and jumped out into the street, feeling like those wandering actors who are driven out of a rich estate in some story one is forced to read in school. On the other hand, in her desperate situation, Alina could not afford to be offended, as to be offended was the prerogative of the rich and well-off.

After a little thought she calmed herself down and decided to change her location. She would wait in the lobby of one of the luxurious hotels in the square, where the doormen don't question who walks in. Since the embassy was directly across, she could sit and watch all day.

What exactly Alina was hoping to see, she herself didn't know, but her instinct told her not to venture far from this place. If she just stayed and watched, something would happen.

She calculated that if she was extremely frugal, she should have enough money for two weeks, as Greece was indeed an inexpensive country. In case she needed to go home, Alina had set aside four hundred dollars for tickets for the possible return. Alina knew that freight traffic between Greece and Israel was not prohibited yet. Perhaps she could manage to be a passenger on one of those ferries to Ashdod or perhaps even get a job on such a ship to earn extra money.

Alina really wanted to return home, and Israel had undoubtedly become her home—hot, open to all the ever-changing winds, which meant dangerous at times, but still her home—and if it were not for the need to find Ron, no one could have stopped her. After all it was better to share the bitter fate and hardships of war with your loved ones, than to hover like ghosts in cities and towns where you were faceless and no one needed you.

But returning to Israel meant losing hope of learning any news about her son for a very long time, because there were no diplomatic relations between Israel and Lebanon. You couldn't even make a phone call to find out information. Her other option was to fly to Germany, where she could at least find a job if she had a place to live. Alina had Vlad's address. Jacques had given her his brother's address at the last minute. She ruminated on how kind Jacques had been, like his mother, and remembering her friends, Alina felt the sharp pang of knowing how truly alone she was now.

Chapter Twelve

ON THE THIRD DAY after the shameful expulsion from the Turkish café, something finally happened. She had already spent a day at the Meridian and another at the Grand Britannia, both of which were in Syntagma Square, as was the embassy. Alina, with her characteristic sense of fashion, easily gave herself the appearance of a bored foreign woman with her daughter. Mashenka's white fur coat, although worn in places, looked quite aristocratic in this southern country. In addition, having cut one of the sweaters which Sofia had given her, Alina made Mashenka a hat with mittens, in which the girl looked like Gerda from the Snow Queen fairy tale. Alina's jeans and sneakers were international tourist clothes (even Princess Diana could have sported them), and a bright handmade scarf, cut from the same sweater, added charm. She and Mashenka did not speak Hebrew—Alina had already learned that refugees from Israel who counted every penny were not popular here, but the great Russian language aroused deep respect among the employees of the luxury hotels.

On the third day they moved to the Hilton. And it was at the Hilton, upon once again returning to warm up after a walk to the Lebanese embassy, that they met Rita—the same Rita who had been at the school which had served as a prison. Rita stepped through the glass doors of the pool area in a terrycloth bathrobe with the hotel logo, looking flushed, evidently having come from the jacuzzi. She held her baby in her arms, and she covered him with a wide fluffy sleeve to protect him from the cold air that issued from the street.

Alina rushed to her as if she were a lifeline, and Rita, oddly enough, was delighted to see Alina as well. Standing near the elevator, Rita immediately began to recount how Khalid had managed to send her and the children to Greece, as she put it, "by diplomatic mail," and the following day had arrived himself. He had barely escaped from Haifa, because after the escape of the hostages—at this Rita looked meaningfully at Alina—he had been in big trouble. But one way or another, they had made it to Greece and had now been here for several weeks. First they had lived in Thessaloniki, and yesterday they had flown to Athens. Khalid had rented an apartment for them, and had hired a man to put it in order. In fact, today after lunch she and her children were moving there.

"Let's go to my room, otherwise the child will freeze, as we're just from the pool," suggested Rita.

Alina didn't want to see Khalid at all, as memories of him were inextricably linked with the dark days of captivity and humiliation. However, even now she was a prisoner of circumstances, and felt no less humiliated by her lack of money and her helplessness. Then it suddenly dawned on Alina that Khalid could help her, as he was Egyptian and therefore could contact the embassy of a friendly Arab country.

This inspiration prompted Alina to rush to Rita without hesitation. What a destiny—to have to turn to this woman for help again and be dependent on her! Alina did not like to be in debt, and even more so to be in debt doubly to the same person. However, there was nothing to be done for it. Perhaps Alina would also be useful to Rita someday.

From the window of Rita's comfortable room, a panorama of the ancient city could be seen. From here, when the twilight hid the ugly working-class districts and the daytime smog dissolved a little, the Acropolis and the Temple of Dionysius, illuminated by wandering spotlights, stood out as bright spots.

Alina stood by the window unable to take her eyes off the view, and listened to Rita.

"Khalid has gone on business, and I will be alone for a week. Listen!" Rita was inspired as she saw Alina by the window. "Why don't you come with me and live with us? I'm so lonely and it's been very hard. I can't even go to the store because of the children. The hotels here are expensive." Rita was convinced that Alina must also be staying at the Hilton. "Come with me! Why waste your money? You'd be better off buying yourself something Greek. Gold, for example, is very valuable. And your daughter will be happier," she nodded towards Mashenka, who had already crouched down to Maya's suitcase of toys.

"And Khalid?" Alina kept her cool. She would never confess to Rita where she actually was living and the state of her finances!

"I'm sure he would only be happy for me, that I'm not alone. I'm serious! The apartment has two floors: a kitchen, a salon and four bedrooms. I'll go crazy there! Khalid comes for three days and then leaves. He's found business partners in Greece. By the way, he's seen some Israelis here with whom he once worked, and you know what it's like these days. Please come with me!"

Alina decided that she would not compel Rita to beg any longer, in case she might suddenly change her mind. To some extent, Alina felt like a real adventurer, but in reality she had no choice.

"I have ordered a taxi for four o'clock." Having received Alina's consent, Rita did not hide her joy. "You should check out and then come here with your things at three. You will stay with the children while I go check out."

"Can Mashenka stay here until three? I need to do something in the city." Alina did not want to drag the child into the cold again.

"Of course, look how well they play! It's just so fortunate that we met!" Rita moved to kiss Alina, but at the last moment backed away in shyness.

At three o'clock, having paid the owner of her hotel and trying not to look at his friend leering at her from behind a fan of cards, Alina returned to the Hilton. On the way, she refused to think about all that constantly plagued her—the war, the alarmed voices over the loudspeakers and the civil defense exercises, or how she still needed to beg Khalid to inquire at the Lebanese embassy on her behalf.

Instead, Alina dreamed of how she would give Masha a nice hot bath and how she herself would take a really hot shower, and then she would feed her daughter a savory broth from a chicken which she had just bought in a shop near her hotel.

Khalid returned a week later. He didn't recognize Alina, whom Rita introduced as an old school friend.

In a baggy gray suit, the lawyer did not look as valiant as in a military uniform, and the mustache really didn't suit him. Still, behind the thick lenses of his glasses, his light brown eyes sparkled with joy, and his puffy lips were demarcated by a distinct rim, which would have been more suitable on a woman.

Alina examined him with curiosity, trying to determine what it was about this man that could arouse such a powerful love. "I love him wildly," Alina remembered Rita's words.

Then Alina caught herself and lowered her eyes. Her curiosity, this greedy interest in people, would lead to no good. Wasn't it enough that she'd just had an incident with that fat Greek—or was he a Turk—in the hotel? This was not the time to provoke Rita's jealousy.

Alina herself was insanely jealous, and didn't allow any woman to approach her husband, regardless of age or appearance, even if she needed, for example, just to find out what time it was. This grotesque jealousy, which lingered like a lasting side-effect of the flu, was a consequence of her unsuccessful first marriage, and she had not found a cure for it yet…

"Today we are invited to a reception at the Lebanese embassy," Rita jabbed Alina's side, nudging her to speak.

"I'll be happy to sit with the children," Alina muttered, and, unable to hold back her tears, ran to the bathroom.

Rita hurried after her. "I'll talk to him on the way! Don't cry. I'm sorry. I thought it would be better if you explained the situation."

"Don't pay me any attention." Alina dabbed her eyes with a wet towel. "This is just nerves."

The evening dragged on unbearably long. The children were bathed and put to bed, the dishes washed, and the linen washed. Then she washed the floor for the second time. Alina was not able to stop for a minute. Finally there was the sound of the door opening, and Alina hurried to the entranceway.

Rita avoided looking Alina in the eye, and Khalid, noticing Alina's agitation, announced from the doorway that Israeli Arab-Christians were transported to Lebanon the day after their arrival, under the auspices of a Christian mission. In the morning, the ambassador would be sending the mission an inquiry about Louise, and they should receive an answer in two weeks.

Alina's legs gave way. From the first day of her arrival in Athens, as she walked around the city with Mashenka, she had looked closely at passers-by in the hope of seeing Louise and Ron. In every curly-haired black-eyed woman she saw Louise, and in every boy she saw Ron. And as she had warmed herself in the hotels, it had always been with a double purpose. All the time it had seemed to her that at any moment she could run into them.

It was impossible to think of a more unfortunate place for them to be than Lebanon. Israel had no diplomatic relations with its northern neighbor; instead there were constant clashes at the border, mutual isolation and hatred. Trying to go there with an Israeli passport was the same as trying to go to the moon—absolutely unrealistic. But it made no sense to stay in Greece much longer, although she would wait for the response from the embassy, and she wouldn't know that for two weeks.

Alina lost heart. She practically didn't leave the apartment, which was so different from the first week she had lived with

Rita, when they had all climbed all the tourist sites, dragging along the baby tucked under the duvet in the stroller. Later in the evenings Alina had read to the girls from The Myths of Ancient Greece, trying to convey to them her childhood love for the exploits of Hercules and the travels of Odysseus. Alina's money was melting away in full accordance with her calculations. They had managed to stretch it out for such a long time only because she no longer paid for housing. The remaining four hundred dollars could be spent on tickets, but to where?

When the two weeks of painful waiting finally ended, Khalid brought disappointing news—among the Christians sent to Lebanon, close or distant relatives had given shelter to the unfortunate refugees, and it was now impossible to find anyone. The search would take an indefinite period.

Khalid and Rita sat opposite Alina, holding hands, and it seemed they were the embodiment of her childhood fantasies—that a day would come when faith, skin color and language would cease to separate people. She had been a humanist, this little girl version of Alina with her dreamy eyes and her beloved Uncle Tom's Cabin… Why did she now sometimes shout "Death to the Arabs?"

"We're leaving for Germany." Khalid reached for coffee from the cezve, and Rita lurched forward to fulfill his desire. "I think you should come with us. Firstly, the children have become very good friends, and you and Rita get along well. She would not be so lonely, and I will try to contact the Lebanese embassy in Munich. An old friend of mine works there. I think he can help."

And Oksana is also there, and I can earn some money, Alina mused to herself, and without wasting time on further thoughts, she agreed. "It's decided, let's go!" Alina stated emphatically. Then she pulled from her pocket the four hundred dollars set aside for tickets and handed them to Khalid.

He didn't realize that going to Germany had been an option before he had suggested it. It only remained to sell the gold she had originally given to Oksana for Mashenka, as she would need something to survive on when she first arrived.

And it would be safer to travel accompanied by Khalid than alone, considering what was happening in Germany.

"Yes," Khalid seemed to have guessed Alina's thoughts, "in Europe the situation seems to be starting to improve. In England, the Prime Minister, despite the fact that he is a Muslim himself, has changed the law on emigration, which has hurt his own people." There was contempt in Khalid's voice. "In France, banks began to suffer losses. So the French, dissatisfied with the pro-Arab sentiments of bankers, as well as out of solidarity with their northern neighbors, began to transfer their savings to Switzerland. An agreement has been concluded in Belgium, with America applying pressure, and the hostages should be released in a week. Only in Germany, where Muslims, dissatisfied with the tightening of policies in other European countries, have begun to gather, is the party of Islam gaining strength. The only thing that can stop it is the discontent of the German people who are finding themselves out of work due to the increase in cheap labor.

"As for Israel," Khalid's eyes fired up at the sore subject, "in Israel everything will happen last. Don't you see who benefits from this complete isolation in the first place? The Israelis! While the whole world is buzzing and worrying, I'm sure your government is slowly putting things in order in the occupied territories of Palestine. They don't want the world noticing, so they will take their time. So you girls have no need to hurry, as it will not be possible to return home soon." Khalid looked at Rita and his face darkened as he remembered that sooner or later he would have to return her to her husband.

"And what about these Muslim detachments?" Alina asked out of turn, just wanting to change the subject; but Khalid froze and Rita's face dropped, as she poured the last drops of coffee with cardamom from the cezve. Alina realized she had blurted out something wrong. Khalid nevertheless answered her, albeit very reluctantly. "These fabricated Muslim detachments are, in essence, mercenaries who are paid and directed by one millionaire from Kuwait with a Napoleon complex. Recruitment is carried out via the internet. One puts in their data and bank account number. And then you get an email invite to train in special camps located … in various places, for example, in Jordan. However, many people who are already trained, who know how to handle weapons and are physically fit, also go there."

Khalid winced, remembering what the camp had been like. Then, realizing he had been carried away by his recollections, he stopped talking and lit a cigarette, without asking permission from the women.

The conversation crumpled, and Alina, feeling herself superfluous, took her cup of coffee and went upstairs to Mashenka, counting the steps, which were richly decorated with wood. The apartment belonged to some Greek diplomat who preferred foreign cold Europe to his native warm Greece, and now would be stuck in Europe for a long time.

Khalid was afraid, thought Alina with malevolent satisfaction, afraid that he would have problems with his Israeli and European business partners once this was over. Even knowing what had made Khalid join these ill-fated squads, namely to rescue Rita, Alina still could not forgive him for her humiliation at the school, and her dependence on him now.

At night, Alina woke up several times and, when the sky finally began to turn gray, foreshadowing the imminent dawn, she gave up and decided to get up. She quietly left the apartment, trying not to wake anyone up, and ran to a jewelry store, Zolotas, in front of whose window she and Rita had stopped several times. The store was, of course, still closed, despite the fact that in Athens, as in all southern cities, the business morning began early in order to capture the coolness of the morning hours.

Annoyed at her foolishness, Alina decided to call Germany so as not to waste time, but again she hadn't reckoned on the time and therefore woke up Vlad, with whom she had never spoken before. The conversation was forced as Alina struggled with the few English phrases she could think of, but the main thing was that Vlad had heard from Oksana and Jacques and they were in Frankfurt. Since Vlad lived in Munich, Alina and Vlad agreed that she would call him when she arrived in Munich, and Alina perked up again.

Returning to Zolotas, she noticed that the owner had already brewed himself a cup of coffee. Alina spread out the contents of a bag filled with rings and earrings on the counter.

The jewelry had mainly sentimental value to her: this ring with a small pomegranate was bought when Alina had just started dating her beloved; and that one, with a diamond which was quite expensive, was his farewell, before he decided to marry someone completely different.

But these small earrings with turquoise the color of her son's eyes were given to her after Ron's birth. Alina had only one earring—the second remained in Ron's bag. She decided to keep this one earring, snatching it at the last moment from the scale where her jewelry had been neatly laid out by the plump hands of the jeweler. Grimacing a little, as she was already unaccustomed to them, Alina put the earring on, while rolling her wrist at the Greek, who smiled contemptuously at her meagre treasure. "Get on with it," her hands said for her, "just count the bills out."

Chapter Thirteen

IN THE ULTRA-MODERN MUNICH airport, Alina immediately felt comfortable, as she always did in Europe. But her
pleasure was poisoned by the thought that she was in Germany, a country she had refused to visit on a principle which she
held sacred and to which she had always adhered.

This feeling came from the depths of her gut. It had been
cultivated by films about World War II, as well as her grandmother's stories about her first-born, Alina's uncle, whom the
Nazis had thrown into a well alive when the child was only
five years old. Yad Vashem, the holocaust museum in Jerusalem, and stories about the Warsaw ghetto, and many other
things that were not widely known in the Soviet Union only
deepened the hatred.

Alina was not alone in feeling this antipathy for Germany.
Many Israelis, some even younger than Alina, basically refused
to buy anything made in Germany, including the world's most
reliable cars. And one elderly professor, the son of emigrants
from Germany, whom Alina had heard about from her friend
Yoram, participated in the Haganah, and said that whenever
he was in Germany at scientific conferences, he would never
shake hands with anyone over fifty, because they could have
been Nazis.

Several generations would need to pass before the memory
of the horrors of Nazism would be erased. On the other hand,
human memory could be short. Perhaps, if others besides

Jews had remembered this cruelest of wars, the world would not be on the verge of a new war now.

On the way into the city, Alina clung to the taxi window and, following Khalid's comments, looked at the wide avenues of Munich, noticing how her curiosity prevailed over her hostility and prejudice. She had expected the city to be gray and boring. Instead Munich reminded her of Italy, with its pompous arches and colonnades. The city astounded her with its unexpected splendor.

Khalid and Rita were heading to the Hilton, and Alina, while still on the plane, had warned them that she would spend the night with friends. Her friends actually lived in Frankfurt, but she couldn't give up the entire proceeds from the sale of the "family jewels" for two nights at the Hilton! Then again, she mused, if her husband were here... If she could spend those two nights with her husband, then ... what she wouldn't give...

By a sheer effort of will, Alina forced herself to switch back to reality. The reality was this: in the evening she would have to take Mashenka and go look for a cheap refuge, and lie that her friends had come for her.

But as soon as their group entered through the automatically parting doors of the hotel, a red fiery mane in an orange jacket with fox trim rushed to Alina. Oksana! Her friend gave the impression of a living fire. Alina noticed out of the corner of her eye how Rita instinctively tried to block Khalid's view, while Khalid stared dumbfounded at this fiery phenomenon.

Davidik hugged Mashenka, and she immediately began to whisper something in his ear. Davidik was still at that happy age when girls were not enemies, but, on the contrary, were preferable to boys in all respects.

Alina, dazed with joy, interrogated Oksana, from whom she learned that Okasana had heard from Vlad that Alina would be at the Hilton. Alina was pleasantly amazed, having completely forgotten that she had told Vlad about the Hilton.

Fifteen minutes later, Alina, having received a promise from Khalid that he would visit the Lebanese embassy tomorrow and having kissed Rita goodbye, rushed with Oksana in her brand new Volkswagen somewhere—it seemed to her—out of town. At first, the children laughed in the back seat, inventing some kind of ear-pulling game, and then unexpectedly quickly fell asleep, as only young children can do.

Oksana, confidently handling the clutch, although she used to drive only automatics in Israel, said, "This car is specially designed for the disabled. It's a manual, so I had to pass the exam. Jacques is in the hospital. He's had a second operation. Now we need to get the money for the third, which will be the last one, and he will become a totally abled person again!"

Alina did not ask who had paid for the operation and where she had found the money to rent a house in the suburbs, not to mention such "little things" as her car or the large screen computer Oksana had mentioned with a built-in video camera. Oksana was wearing a set of older earrings, which had been given to her by David. So Alina asked something completely different:

"And what about David?"

For some reason, Oksana began her reply by referring to her husband. "You know, Mishka and I lived like a cat and a dog. He was always criticizing me—my figure was bad, my nose too long. I got into a scandal the day before the wedding. I wanted to run away from the wedding, but my mother wouldn't let me. But I didn't love him anymore. Then I fell in love with various men, several times, but more and more so, platonically.

"David was my first lover after my husband, and you know how hard he tried to get me. He gave me a job; he always supported me in so many ways. Of course, he's not handsome. I wouldn't say that he is, but I became attached to him. I have never known a more romantic love in my life. And when Davidik was born," Oksana smiled, casting a glance in the rearview mirror at her sleeping son. "After five daughters what does a son mean for an Iraqi Jew? Need I say more?

"The only thing that upsets David is that he cannot give his son his last name, and Davidik will not inherit his father's fortune." Oksana chuckled to herself, fully aware of the less than substantial inheritance. "The child, of course, brought us very close, but, you know, we worked together, we had a child together—and love?

"He stopped telling me that I was his star, the moon that illuminated his path, a long time ago... He removed all the classic pictures of red-haired beauties by masters such as Renoir, which he had hung in his office when we first met, claiming that they reminded him of me. And lately we've been making love once a week, sometimes less often. And no longer in a hotel, but right there, in the office, on the table. Very 'romantic.' More importantly, it doesn't cost any money. In short, this relationship has long since fizzled out. And now, when I finally fell in love... "

"And what about Dzhabril?" Alina decided to change the subject, especially since they were already turning into the driveway. Oksana pulled the car into the spacious garage, and the friends carefully pulled out their sleeping children, deciding to get the luggage later.

"Dzhabril," Oksana puffed under the weight of Davidik who was snoring, "Dzhabril is here, and Katya too. They went for groceries and will be back soon."

"What?" Alina stumbled and almost dropped Mashenka. "Do they live in Germany now?"

"Well, no! Dzhabril was recruited to work with the Red Cross in Lebanon, and Katya was as well. But their entry was delayed due to the war. So they are staying here until they can leave. As you probably heard, the situation is starting to improve, and maybe," Oksana's voice trembled, "my girls will finally be able to come to me... "

Alina wasn't listening anymore. "Lebanon? So Dzhabril and Katya are flying to Beirut?"

"Yes, in three days. Why are you suddenly so excited? And I didn't get a chance to ask—why isn't Ron with you?"

"Exactly! Because he is in Lebanon!"

Unable to carry the sleeping children to the second floor, Alina and Oksana put them on the leather sofa in the living room, and then went into the kitchen. Oksana started making coffee.

"Ron is in Lebanon with Louise, and I don't know anything about them. No leads." Alina began to sniffle, as she always did when she started talking about Ron.

"Well, you see, now everything will be settled! Don't cry. Dzhabril will find them. And here they are!"

Oksana hadn't had time to say anything about her sister, but at first glance it was clear that these two were together and happy.

As if anticipating Alina's questions, Katya, having just greeted them, said, "I left my children with my mother until we get settled."

It was evident that the separation from the children tormented Katya, and it pained her to have to explain the situation over and over again.

Alina smiled at her. "You did the right thing. They need to graduate from school and get their diplomas. Lebanon is not the best place."

"Not Lebanon, but Libya," Dzhabril meticulously corrected, noticeably plumper on Ukrainian dumplings.

"Libya?" Alina asked, confused. "Aren't you flying to Beirut?"

"Yes, through Beirut, to Libya, to treat the president," Dzhabril chuckled.

"Why the president?" Alina asked mechanically, depressed by Oksana's stupid mistake.

"Because, as I understand it, there is only one hospital—the presidential one."

"And we will open another one, for ordinary people!" Katya put in, in a voice full of youthful enthusiasm.

Everyone smiled at her naive optimism. Katya was no longer young. She was an adult woman, but after spending her whole life in a confined space—her home, with her children and her disabled husband—part of her had somehow remained a sixteen-year-old girl.

Unpacking about ten boxes of prepared salads and cold cuts, Katya—who had never allowed herself to buy these things in Ukraine, although ready-made dishes had begun to appear there—insisted that Alina and Oksana join the meal.

They quickly finished their impromptu feast, and "the young," as Katya and Dzhabril were jokingly referred to by Oksana, slipped into a luxurious bedroom, incapable of getting fed up with either the bedroom or each other. When they were left alone, Alina, dejected by yet another failure of the "Lebanese operation," did not want to talk. But Oksana, apparently wanting to distract her friend from her sadness, or perhaps feeling the need to relieve her soul, began, as always, decisively. "You, of course, must have guessed where the money for the operation came from."

"Yes. I understand. I only pray to God that you don't get caught."

There are unsolved crimes, she told herself, unable to label Oksana with the weighted word "criminal." In truth, she didn't condemn her friend. Rather, she admired her determination to cross the line, not so much the line of the law as the line of Oksana's own notions of decency.

Wasn't decency an inner conviction that not a single act will go unpunished, and that all your actions will return to you like a boomerang—both good and bad?

"I know," Oksana seemed to read Alina's thoughts. "I understand that I will pay for this, as I will pay for leaving David, and my husband… " She stopped Alina with a wave of her hand, as Alina tried to interject at the word husband. "Yes, and I am guilty in my marriage. I should not have clung to him, not been afraid to be alone back then, in my youth… Living with a person you annoy is provoking him to show the most unpleasant parts of his nature. But it is doubly criminal,"

Oksana used the same word in a different context than Alina, and here it was more appropriate, "to live with a person who annoys you! I will have to pay for everything either in this life or there," she raised her eyes to the ceiling, "but I will never regret what I did for Jacques!"

"Love justifies everything." Alina tried to reduce the pathos of her friend's monologue into a common phrase.

"Yes, love!" Oksana picked up the phone and vigorously began to dial a number, making it clear that the topic was closed. Although she sometimes frightened Alina with her frankness in the most delicate matters, Oksana was usually bashful in conversations about romance.

Alina volunteered to accompany her friend to the hospital to see Jacques, despite the fact that her eyes were drooping after a hard day. Although she was not a lover of detective stories, she nevertheless couldn't suppress the desire to find out all the details of "the case of the glittering earrings."

"Do you remember that red-faced taxi driver who drove us to Brashev?" In the car, Oksana spoke more openly, because Katya knew nothing about the story with the earrings, thinking that all the "wealth" came from Jacques.

"Of course." Alina remembered how her insides were shaking from fear on the serpentine Carpathian Mountains, especially when she saw the exits to country roads leading to distant abandoned farms.

"He exchanged the earrings for real diamonds while we were still at the airport. He did it so cleverly that you didn't even notice, and I was to stay a week at the boarding house to ensure that I wasn't being followed. I didn't say a word at the time, so as not to bring all this up again, but then you must remember what happened.

"When the news reported the exposure of a criminal group and the jeweler was arrested, the taxi driver showed up one evening to take the diamonds back. You had just left Poiana Brashev, and they wanted to abort the plan. They no longer needed me, but now I needed them.

"I offered to take the diamonds to Germany, I didn't care anymore. He was very surprised at my willingness, as it was clear that I was no criminal, but in principle he liked this turn of events. So he asked what I wanted for it…

"And you can guess what happened next. They paid for the operation, rented a house for us near the clinic for two months, and put several thousand dollars in the bank."

"I would have asked for more," Alina chuckled.

"I have no magic lamp, nor a Djinn to grant me wishes." Oksana took a pack of Marlboros out of her bag, pulled out a cigarette and, sighing, put it back into the pack. "And I quit smoking. Jacques is allergic."

Alina could not believe her ears. Oksana smoked even when she was "in a delicate condition," although she was tormented by remorse, and after each cigarette swore that it would be her last. And now, really—this is what made her quit!

"And what's next?" Alina asked.

"What's next?"

"When you run out of money and rent."

"Who cares?" The same Oksana who earlier would panic at any change, or even uncertainty, shrugged her shoulders nonchalantly. "Something will happen. One thing I can tell you with certainty though. I will remain with Jacques."

Chapter Fourteen

AFTER A LONG JOURNEY ALONG the dark highway, Alina's eyes slowly became accustomed to the bright neon lights of the hospital corridor, and the dazzling whiteness of the walls, furniture, and even the staff's dressing gowns. The first person Alina saw in the hospital lobby was, of all people … Gosha. Oksana had rushed after an orderly—a puny, eastern-looking man with oiled curls. In general, the junior medical personnel were not of Aryan origin. But Gosha—tall, fair-haired, with blue eyes betraying his Latvian roots—looked like a perfect German.

Alina was frightened by his sunken eyes and taut cheekbones. In a month and a half since their separation at the Haifa airport, he had lost a lot of weight and, in general, looked ill. "What are the chances? How did you get here?" Alina asked him.

They were neither lovers, nor relatives, nor even friends, but somehow their paths crossed at the most difficult crossroads of their destinies.

Years ago, Irina, Alina's client and Gosha's beloved, had died almost before Alina's eyes, and after her death, knowing that she had died precisely because of him, Gosha had abandoned both his restaurant and a bar he ran for foreign sailors. Years later, Alina and Gosha had met at the prison school where Alina had been a hostage, and Gosha had been the mayor of the abandoned city, which meant he was practically the only official left. Since then, they had both walked on a razor's edge.

And now, they were meeting when Alina was at a complete dead end in terms of reuniting with her son, and Gosha, it turned out, was terminally ill. He told her immediately, as was customary among the Israelis and, in general, in the West. Alina still found this surprising, as in the Soviet Union the terminally ill were never told they were dying, and they didn't readily reveal this information if they found out.

"Is that why you left Haifa?" she asked.

"Not really… You see, strange things started happening. Almost immediately after you flew away, I was shot at twice, and then the front door of my house was blown off with explosives. I realized that this was a warning. It was time to dump everything. After all, how long can one go on fighting windmills? Moreover, I was really beginning to feel sick. I was losing weight and sleeping poorly. I needed a medical examination. And where could I get one in Israel? Hospitals only operate for the army now. So in one day I was able to pack up and fly away, knowing my wife would be okay, as she is staying with our daughter in Jerusalem outside the military zone."

"How did you fly to Germany?"

"Moscow flight. I asked them to stop in Frankfurt," Gosha answered casually, as if he had requested a stop from a taxi driver. Then, being frank, or maybe just wanting to boast, he added, "Do you remember that my sister has a charter company in Moscow? I made sure that her planes could land in Haifa, as I have connections… And this when Israel isn't accepting any commercial planes at all, especially in the north. So there's a lot of money to be made off this."

And you also got your cut, thought Alina, as she said aloud, "I had already decided that you work for the Russians, hence your connections…"

"I work only for myself. Although now, it seems my work is done… You and Marina?"

"I'm with Oksana. Her friend was operated on here. Did you know each other in Haifa?"

Oksana was just returning to them, having finally let go of the orderly, who had exhausted his stock of English words. Gosha glanced at her indifferently and turned away, so unlike before, when at the sight of any woman he would perk up, begin to bow, kiss her hands and generally fan out his bright plumage. Alina felt sad, only now realizing how indifferent he already was to everything that connected him with life. But as it turned out, not everything.

"And Marina?" he asked again.

"Marina stayed in Ternopil. Do you want her phone number?" Alina burst out.

Oksana pinched her hand, but it was too late. Gosha was already pulling a pen out of his breast pocket, and Alina didn't have time to think of an excuse or claim forgetfulness So instead she asked cautiously, "What will you do with it?"

"I want Marina to come here. I will pay her to be my nurse." For some reason Gosha focused only on Alina, although Oksana was standing next to her. "You know, they say that sincerely loving someone means wanting to grow old with that person. So I want to grow old with Marina. She won't have to wait long… I've realized that I came into this world only for the sake of these few months, which, if possible, I'd like to spend with her."

Gosha's words may have been reminiscent of a cheap melodrama, but there was sincerity in his tone. Oksana, who was long overdue to go to Jacques, especially since Gosha was not even noticing her, could not bring herself to budge.

"I didn't believe in these feelings before… " Gosha continued.

He paused, unable to cope with his sentiments, his jaw clenched.

"Do you remember Irina, and how she literally came between me and the knife meant to kill me? She always told me that she loved me, but only now do I realize what love really is. Since the day of your departure, there has not been a day that I did not think about Marina, but then I told myself I could wait. Now I count the minutes of my life. They, like sand in an hourglass, are continuously being poured down the hole, leaving less and less time on the surface… If I can see Marina, this will probably be the last gift from the Fates."

Oksana silently took the pen from Gosha and wrote Marina's phone number on the back of some hospital form.

Alina could not believe her eyes. She knew how Oksana was afraid of Marina showing up, since Marina was predatory in enticing other women's men. What would it matter to her that Jacques was disabled? All he would have to do is look at Marina, and not Oksana, and the outcome would be the same. On this Alina had no doubts. She knew that she could rely on Marina in hard times, but only because there was no man present.

Gosha neatly folded the sheet with the coveted number. His excitement subsided. The blush, which had revived his thin face for a moment, disappeared, and Gosha again seemed tired, sick and hopelessly old.

To change the subject, Alina began to recount that she couldn't locate her son, although she realized that a person with one foot in the next world may already be indifferent to earthly affairs, especially those of strangers. However, when he heard about Lebanon, he perked up and said that one friend for whom he had gotten passage out of Haifa on the last plane was a Christian Arab. This man was in Frankfurt, waiting for the return of his wife and children tomorrow, who were in Lebanon with relatives.

Alina suddenly felt like she was on a roller coaster, as her heart plummeted.

"Gosh," she said hoarsely. "What's his name?"

"Angelo Amelek, and his wife Louise."

"It's them, Gosha!" Alina shouted, as she went to squeeze Gosha in her arms, then immediately pulled herself back, remembering his condition.

"What are you afraid of?" Gosha chuckled. "Don't bury me before my time. I'm still alive. I can still do something… And now," he waved the leaflet with Marina's phone number in front of Alina, "now I have hope."

"Goshenka, how can I find them?" Alina could no longer think or talk about anything else.

"I told you—he is in Frankfurt, at the Forum Hotel. Here's the address. Here's the phone number. Hurry up."

"And you, where will you be?"

"I'll be here," Gosha smiled weakly. "I don't know how long it will take, but I won't go anywhere. Don't worry."

Knowing she should be polite, she sought out Jacques' ward, but he greeted her without enthusiasm, perhaps fearing she was a bad influence on Oksana. Alina hardly noticed though, as her mind was already focused on hurrying home to pick up Mashenka and rush to Frankfurt.

"Where? What are you thinking?" Oksana tried to restrain her friend's fervor. "There are no trains or buses at night!"

"I'll take a taxi!" Alina blurted out, but then remembered her dire financial situation and bit her tongue.

"You're not going anywhere! Vlad arrives in the morning. He has business in Munich, and in the afternoon he'll return to his home in Frankfurt. You will go with him in his car. It will be more convenient, cheaper, and it will be more entertaining for him. Until then, call the hotel, talk to Angelo, and calm down."

Despite the late hour, Alina, obsessed with the idea, began to call and all but harass the receptionists who were on night duty at the Forum. Yet, despite the receptionists' efforts, it became clear that no one was answering in Angelo's room.

Walking … on the last night without his wife, Alina wondered and then was immediately ashamed of her thoughts.

After several wonderful years with her second husband, she once again believed that there was a place for love and fidelity in a long marriage, so why deprive others of this trust? Then this thought led to another, which was that she was worried about tomorrow's trip with Vlad. Alina's husband, as jealous as she was, had skillfully instilled in her that every man who happened to be around was a potential enemy, who dreamt of encroaching on her honor.

She knew it was silly, but an awkward feeling remained with her, buzzing about her like an annoying fly, until the next morning when Alina met Vlad.

Vlad, so smart and educated, whose voice had struck her in their telephone conversation as both courageous and tender, turned out to be a short, thin man, with a whitish corolla of curly hair like Mikhail's, framing a pale bald patch. With a small, constantly smiling face, small nose and plump wet lips, he was somewhat reminiscent of a Disney gnome, only without a cap. Alina sighed with relief.

His English was simple, like in a comic book; and when Vlad, without any embarrassment, said that he was living with a friend, but that Alina and Mashenka could spend the night in their living room, this calmed her down even more.

After having breakfast and saying goodbye to Dzhabril and Katya, Alina kissed Oksana, who thrust several crumpled bills into her palm. Without the usual "you shouldn't" and "I can't accept," Alina simply took the money, whispering "thank you" through welling tears. She threw a bag of things into the trunk of a worn out Opel, and sat with Mashenka in the back seat. Then, committing what in her opinion was the height of indecency, she slept all the way to Frankfurt.

"We've arrived," Vlad woke her at the entrance to a modern building. "The Hotel Forum. Go check if your Angel is in the room." Vlad pronounced the name funny, as they would in Romanian. "We'll wait here in the car."

Alina went up to the tenth floor, having learned the room number from the night porter, but no one answered her knock.

He's not there, she thought, as she went down past the lobby to the car. Though dejected, Alina tried to make a joke, struggling to find the right English words. "He seems to exist, but in fact he doesn't."

Vlad thought quickly. "Go ask the receptionist to call the airport and find out when the plane arrives from Beirut. Stop! Better wait here. I'll find out myself."

Vlad returned a few minutes later with an encouraging smile. "Tomorrow at noon. So there is nothing to worry about until tomorrow. For now we are going to my place."

They drove along the bypass road and returned to the city again, to the old district of stone houses from the late nineteenth century with stucco facades and impossibly steep narrow stairs. Alina scrambled up to the top floor with difficulty. Fortunately Mashenka, who had never woken up, was carried by Vlad, who, as it turned out, possessed remarkable strength for his stubby physique.

The apartment, or rather studio, as it was called in Europe, consisted of a kitchen and living room, which simultaneously served as the entrance hall. Past a door one could guess was a bedroom, which had an area fenced off by a curtain for the "amenities." It was the unusual arrangement of the toilet that Alina felt gave a peculiar charm to these shelters of students, emigrants, and such semi-legal couples as Vlad and his "friend," who barely said "bonjour" and then disappeared again.

Contrary to the widespread stereotype that in homosexual couples it is always clear who dominates, Alina couldn't tell anything like that about her new acquaintances. Vlad's partner was just as short and rather fragile looking. His head was adorned with exuberant black hair, which made Alina think he must be of Middle Eastern origin. Thick eyebrows, converging on the bony bridge of his nose, were black as shoe polish, but the lower part of his face ended with an elegant mouth and a soft capricious chin, as if the upper and lower halves of the face belonged to different people.

A few minutes later, Vlad left the bedroom, closing the door tightly, and, looking away, mumbled, choosing simple and understandable words for Alina in English:

"You won't be able to spend the night here." He gestured to the bedroom door. "He is jealous."

Alina furrowed her brow at this English word which she didn't understand. So Vlad pantomimed strangulation. Alina laughed, and the awkwardness that they both felt dissipated. Having cheered up a bit, Vlad took Mashenka in his arms and said with a wink, "Let's go. I know where you will spend the night."

As they went down the stairs, Alina tried to find out why his friend was jealous if Vlad wasn't interested in women.

"Who says I'm not interested?" Vlad laughed and gave Alina such a look that she no longer wanted to ask questions.

Twenty minutes later, Vlad pulled up on the sidewalk in front of a door with a playful sign of a bed in the shape of a bikini-clad girl.

A short Chinese woman was on duty at the counter in the entrance, and a little behind her, like a bodyguard, was a giant Black man, apparently a bouncer. "So cosmopolitan!" Alina admired the diversity, as she watched Vlad nod in greeting, and explain something to them, pointing to Alina and Masha, and putting bills on the counter. The impassive, shimmering white face of the Chinese woman and the motionless figure of the Black man, partially illuminated by a dim lamp, gave the place a mysteriously disturbing look, as in a Dickens' novel.

Vlad returned Alina to reality by handing her the key to the room, and not without pride noted that she would be accommodated in a room for especially important guests. Having promised to arrive at ten in the morning to take them to the airport, Vlad began to say goodbye.

"Money! I owe you money!" Alina reached into her pocket.

"No, it's taken care of," Vlad dismissed her. "Goodbye."

He headed for the car.

Alina climbed the stairs sideways, for some reason afraid to turn her back on the couple behind the counter, and reached the second floor while firmly holding Mashenka's hand, who was finally awake.

The VIP room consisted of two parts. In the first there was a couch and a table, and further in, on a special dais, a huge double bed was solemnly located, with a lace bedspread and plaster angels above the headboard.

The angels' noses were flaky and one wing was broken off. Red Chinese lanterns were placed on the ground and hung everywhere. The best part of the room was the bathroom which had a floor of transparent plastic tiles, each of which held a light bulb. However, Alina failed to turn on the light, or she would have noticed that the bulbs didn't work. Both the bathtub and the bed were reflected in a huge mirror fixed to the ceiling, in the center of which there was a zigzag crack.

Alina, who until now had never been to such establishments, took a while to realize that the rooms here were intended for a very specific purpose. And, judging by Vlad's relaxed behavior, he was in his element here. Alina could not believe that a man who was basically a beggar, an emigrant from the former "socialist camp," could afford the luxury of "love for hire." Most likely, Vlad worked here part-time. But in what role? Alina didn't pursue this idea though, as she felt it was much more interesting if a person had some kind of secret, its contents sometimes better left unknown.

In the morning, instead of the agreed upon ten o'clock, Vlad arrived closer to eleven, disheveled and looking guilty.

"Sorry, my friend … all night," he started to make excuses, but then remembered that Alina didn't know English well. So he once again pantomimed strangulation, and he was so inspired that as he blushed and coughed, Alina was momentarily scared that Vlad was really strangling himself. He was so sweet and funny, this repentant gnome, that Alina immediately forgave him for the endless hour of anxious waiting, and the delay to the airport.

They walked towards the exit, past the same couple behind the counter. In the daylight, the Chinese woman no longer seemed like a mysterious priestess of the East, but more like the Korean woman in the Kyiv market from whom Alina always bought carrots; and the Black man's face was transformed by the sun into "Uncle Tom," radiating good nature and sympathy.

When Vlad, squeezing all possible and impossible speed from the poor Opel, finally got them to the airport, the plane, as Alina had feared, had already landed. Despite the tightening of customs for all arriving from Arab countries, the passengers on the Beirut flight had been, thanks to the legendary accuracy and pedantry of German officials, safely passed through all the "filters," and having managed to get their luggage, had now scattered in different directions.

Vlad pulled the car from the airport lot with the air of a dashing horseman, turning his horse at full gallop in the excitement of the chase, and drove it back to the Forum Hotel. This time, his gallant efforts were crowned with success. Angelo and Louise Amelek had just arrived, the receptionist reported, pointing to a group of suitcases waiting near the elevator to be sent to their room.

Alina looked frantically at the children's backpacks, which had fallen behind Louise's large leather suitcase, searching among them for Ron's bag—a brand new one, which had been bought for the beginning of the school year. Then she remembered that Ron was a big boy now and preferred not to part with his things, and having calmed down, she pressed the elevator button.

Alina jumped into the room without even knocking, taking advantage of the fact that the door had not yet slammed shut behind the newly entered guests. With a short nod to Louise, who was numb with surprise in the room's hallway, Alina tuned her ears like radar, prepared to snatch her son's high voice from among the sounds emitting from the next room. In her hands she was clutching a bag containing a sweater and jacket, bought on sale in Frankfurt, when she had regretted cutting the sweater Sofia had knit for Ron. The warm winter in Germany was much harsher than the cold winter in Greece.

Contrary to her expectations, no one ran into the hallway and threw themselves around her neck. Finally finding her voice, Louise spoke with a strong accent that perhaps was forged from intense excitement or perhaps came from such a long break from using Hebrew. "Don't you know anything?"

"What?!" Alina's knees buckled and everything seemed to float before her eyes. With sheer will, she drove away her deep-seated fearful thoughts and remained as if in a vacuum, listening to Louise's voice coming from afar through the emptiness that blocked her ears.

Upon arrival in Athens, they had discovered that all Christian Arabs would be transported to Lebanon to be put under the care of the Christian community there. Louise immediately realized what danger this would put Ron in. A child who doesn't speak Arabic, circumcised—it would be madness to take him to the "enemy's lair," to a country where even among the Christian minority there was not a person who didn't burn with hatred for his neighbors.

Louise went mad with anxiety, not knowing what to do with the boy, how to take on such a responsibility. Fortunately for her, among the representatives of the Christian missions who met them in Greece, there was a monk from the Russian monastery of St. Panteleimon, on Holy Mount Athos. Upon hearing Ron humming a Russian song to himself under his breath, the monk showed an interest in the boy.

The monk listened to Louise's fears, and without hesitation offered to shelter the boy in the monastery until his parents could come for him. Elderly, handsome, with intelligent blue eyes, he reminded Louise of a Russian musician who often played the saxophone under the windows of her office. Furthermore, with his monk's gray beard and excellent English, he reminded her of Christmas somehow, and she was comforted by him.

Stunned by the news, Alina stood, leaning her hand against the wall, unable to utter a word. Today's failure was just the last link in a long chain of previous failures. Looking at Louise, she forced herself to think about anything else. She focused on the gold brooch in front of her—the shape of the cross on the lapel of a solid black jacket. The diamonds must be fake, right? Now focus on the second cross resting on Louise's high white chest. Now Angelo's shoes, expensive, though not polished in a long time, and his dark blue suit hanging like a sack from his thin figure...

After rummaging through her tote bag, Louise held out a piece of paper with the monk's name and address, written in English and Russian. "I gave your money and gold to the monk," she added, and continued apologetically, "I was looking for you and your husband all the time. Sent a thousand messages in every way I could, and through Angelo too." Louise tilted her head towards her husband, who was standing next to her, his face so sympathetic.

Previously, Angelo's expression had always seemed arrogant and disgusted to Alina, and only now did it occur to her that in Israel he must have had to be on his guard all the time, since he was taking upon himself both the common hostility towards Arabs and the condescending contempt for Christians. After the collapse of Israel, literally into two camps, Angelo and his family, and other Christian Arabs, did not have a quiet place in either half. Therefore, no matter how joyful the meeting of the spouses and the reunification of children with their father, when the freshness of these sensations dulled, these people would have nowhere to go.

And Alina herself? What would she do with two children in her arms tomorrow, for example, if Ron were here? She finally knew the answer to that question, which she had asked herself more than once, and hadn't wanted to dwell on... She would return... Yes, to the war; yes, with two children ... to where she was afraid to stay ... to where parents, neighbors, friends and just comrades in misfortune were ... next to her husband and sons—for there is where she belonged.

Sometimes it happens that in the most difficult moments something happens that seriously distracts you from your personal experiences, and you suddenly realize that the world does not close around your pain—that you need to exist and act, that life requires your participation. So it happened with

Alina when an agitated Vlad with a mobile phone in his hand looked through the open door of the room and called to her enthusiastically, his voice all but pulling her into the corridor. Alina herself had wanted to leave as soon as possible, as it was so hard for her to witness this happy family.

Mashenka whimpered, tired of the morning's senseless race and the endless standing around in the hallway of this room, where Ron, whom her mother had promised her would appear, did not, causing her to feel sad.

Louise fussed, "Sit down, rest! I have cookies and juice for the kids. You can order pizza."

"No, sorry. It's not possible. He's waiting for us," Alina pointed to Vlad, who, realizing that Louise had not brought Alina's son, froze at the door despite his urgent news. "Thank you, we'll go."

Louise's eyes—large, black, expressive—were filled with tears, and Alina, pushing Vlad sideways through the half-open door, pulled at Mashenka, who, after tearful lamentations of "Cookies, I want cookies!" got one in each hand, and was now reluctant to walk out of the room. Having quickly thanked and kissed Louise goodbye and even, by rote, Angelo, Alina hastily retreated.

She gradually came to her senses, and the feeling of hopeless despair melted within her into a stubborn force, which rose from somewhere in the depths of her chest to her very throat, causing spasms from unshed tears, and bringing all the cells of her body into a state of alertness.

Alina loved this feeling of having a compressed spring inside herself, despite the fact that it was associated with the most difficult moments in her life. And now, full of determination to act, she looked at Vlad, and tensed before the next "English exam," ready for the news, probably about Jacques. But to Alina's surprise, the news was about Oksana.

Taking into account Alina's pitiful knowledge of English, Vlad accompanied his explanations with abundant gestures. His inner actor showed as he proceeded. He used his fingers as bars to mark a prison, and a painfully thrown back head with closed eyes mimed the suffering of Jacques, who had learned that Oksana had been taken to the police. Silent sobs which shook the body of the little man were the tears of Davidik. No matter how funny it was to look at him, the news was alarming, and Alina decided that she had to return to Munich.

Leaving Frankfurt without regret, although she had not even seen the city, Alina suggested first that they go to the hospital, to Jacques. Jacques was so deeply upset that Alina would never have made out his agitated monologue if Vlad had not come along to help.

It turned out that Oksana had been taken away the night before, just after Alina's departure. She had been charged with smuggling, allegedly at the request of the Ukrainian government. Davidik was with her, and had a social worker assigned to him.

If Alina wanted to take the boy, she would have to say that she was Oksana's sister. Then Jacques switched to Romanian to address his brother, who objected angrily and very strongly. They no longer translated for Alina, but she guessed without any translation that Jacques was apparently going to do something in connection with Oksana that was potentially harmful to himself.

Alina was very tired and did not delve further into the family scenario. It wasn't possible to visit Oksana until the morning. So for now it was necessary to figure out where she could stay overnight. Jacques gave Alina his keys, saying that the door was not sealed by the police, and she could live there for another two weeks until the end of the lease.

Vlad volunteered to take them, and dropped her off with Mashenka near the entrance to the garden, then drove off, wishing her luck. Alina had to fight alone with the lock in the gate, alternately warming the key, then her hands, with her breath. After the thaw of the past week, when everyone had walked around without hats in unbuttoned jackets and chuckled that it was warmer in Germany than in Greece, the temperature had dropped again, and fresh snow creaked underfoot. If not for the worries which filled her, including the damned rusted gate to this castle, Alina would have admired the beauty of the frosty trees, illuminated by a clear moon, which also seemed to crackle with frost.

Mashenka, trying not to freeze, broke into the bunny hop dance, accompanying her mother as she tapped at the lock. What happiness the dancing brought, as the child forgot about everything. Finally, surrendering to Alina's sheer stubbornness, the gate opened. The front door also took some time, but eventually capitulated, and Alina burst into the dark hallway. She first rushed to turn on the heat, as thrifty Germans didn't bother to heat their houses if they were absent.

In the morning, Alina went to see Oksana. The German prison was not much like what Alina had imagined from books and films. It was more like a hospital or a school, where instead of doctors or teachers, brave police officers of respectable age were in charge—no matter what they lacked in their pants... With each passing minute, Alina's wait grew sadder. Oksana, on the other hand, went out to Alina cheerfully, as if spending her vacation in a seaside sanatorium.

"It felt like a mountain was lifted from my shoulders," Oksana explained to Alina. "It would have happened eventually. Nothing goes unpunished. But I got Jacques his operation..."

Always Jacques and Jacques... How crazy! No, really, love is akin to illness, thought Alina with sudden irritation. "And Davidik?" she asked, hoping to bring her friend back to reality.

Glimpses of reason appeared in Oksana's eyes. "I said you were my sister. Take him to your place. The apartment is paid for for the next two weeks. We need to find David so that he can come for the child and take him to Israel."

"How can you find him? And how will he come? After all, no one is allowed out of Israel!" said Alina, remembering her own unsuccessful attempts to contact her husband. "And even if David could come, what would he say to his wife and family? They don't know that Davidik is his son. And what about your husband?"

"What? My husband? The idiot can't do anything. David has money, connections. As for the family—there is a war going on, and wars erase the past… "

Alina looked closely at Oksana. Maybe her friend had gone mad from her grief and suffering? No, Oksana looked quite normal. "Well, okay. What will happen to you?"

"I don't know yet. I didn't confess to anything. But in my opinion, they found Ira—the one who gave me the earrings with the fake stones.

"If she points the finger at me, I won't hide that I took the earrings for the purpose of smuggling them; but I will say that, frightened, I didn't meet with anyone and threw them away in Romania. It seems to me that they don't know anything concrete yet, except that, at her request, I left Ukraine for Romania with some earrings. I have no money left for a lawyer. I'll have to do with whoever the court appoints."

Alina rode home with a heavy heart, staring unseeingly out the bus window. She stopped to pick Davidik up from the social worker, and then fell quiet again. Davidik and Mashenka were having fun discussing something in Hebrew. Alina remembered that she had only two days left of money. What to do now? Work? Where? And with whom would she leave the children? Alina wasn't used to asking for a loan. It felt shameful, so shameful… She only had a few acquaintances here: Oksana, Jacques, Vlad, Khalid, Rita…

"Gosha!" It dawned on Alina suddenly. "He can help! And if he can't, I can at least seek his advice on this."

Alina and the children immediately transferred to a bus going to the hospital. The children would have to be left at home next time, as travel was expensive.

Gosha met Alina in a great mood, with a satisfied smile on his pale face, which seemed unnaturally large because of his shaved head. He lay in a separate room, connected by wires and tubes to several devices.

"I decided," he said, "after this examination and the chemotherapy to make a trip around the world. I will choose the mode of transport depending on how much time the German Aesculapians leave me. If they give me a couple of months, I will fly on airplanes. If they give me a couple of years, I will go by ships and trains. I will see the world!" Gosha closed his eyes dreamily.

"Gosh, I came to ask for some money." Alina was not up for standing on ceremony. "And maybe you can come up with some work for me?"

But Gosha, as if not hearing her, continued, "And I will go with Marina. You know she's coming today. I got through. By the way, can you take her girl with you for a while? Marina will be here all the time… There's your job. I'll pay you for it," he concluded, proving he had heard everything.

Alina once again rushed to kiss him. Gosha smiled generously, reached with his free hand to the bedside table, and took out a hundred-dollar bill. With the gesture of a patron he handed it to Alina. "This is for your salary."

It was nice to receive money as part of her salary, and not as a handout, and it was even more pleasant that Gosha had not offered another kind of job—one which had been his specialty at the dawn of their acquaintance, when their offices had been on the same street, and Alina had been a professional astrologer, while Gosha had supplied cheap girls to foreign sailors, and expensive women to his high-ranking friends. Hearing him talk about Marina with the ardor of sixteen-year-old Romeo, no one would have believed that Gosha had once been involved in such matters.

From the day of Marina's arrival, their lives entered into a rut of sorts. Alina lived with Mashenka, Dana and Davidik in the house of Oksana and Jacques. Despite the unconventional situation, their days passed remarkably routinely. In the morning, taking the trodden paths behind the houses, Alina ran to the store for bread and milk. She didn't like to walk along the main streets, allowing all those Fraus and Frauleins to stare at her from behind their starched curtains, as they wondered who she was.

The owner of the shop, an elderly German with a shiny bald head and colorless eyes, silently accepted the money, but behind Alina's back he exchanged glances with his Frau, dissatisfied that Alina always bought so little.

The nearest supermarket was ten minutes away by car, but Alina didn't have a car. All products, except bread and milk, were ordered online from some cheap warehouse with the help of Jacques. Alina cooked and even baked, as she had discovered some recipes for pies and cookies in an old Russian-language newspaper that Oksana had left lying around.

Thanks to the fact that Jacques bought almost all the groceries, and her own scrimping, Alina was able to gradually save some money to return to Greece. Yet, precisely because she still didn't have enough for the trip, and the Greek embassy had still not answered her, Alina was in that limbo state that you experience at a resort or in a hospital—although the days count down, it's the small daily tasks and inane questions which occupy the mind fully, as if these were the most important issues of your life.

Currently Alina's main concern was how to feed, clean and keep three children occupied. Every other day she took the bus to the hospital, sometimes bringing homemade pies for Jacques, Gosh and Marina. The days when she didn't go to the hospital were dedicated to Oksana, to whom Alina went with Davidik, leaving the girls at home. These trips were called "visiting your mother in the hospital," and Alina showed her skills in resourcefulness when she had to explain to the boy why his mother and uncle Jacques were being treated in different hospitals.

Oksana refused the pies, complaining that she had already gained three extra pounds on the nourishing prison food and now she had to work them off in the gym—a new facility and a source of pride for the only man in the institution, the ever-drunk head of the prison, who reminded Alina of Karl Marx without a beard.

Several times Rita and her children came to visit in a rented Mercedes, and once she left the kids with Alina to spend the night, since Khalid had been invited to some kind of reception. From her, Alina learned the latest news. Alina and her children only watched cartoons, since they didn't know German and Alina had difficulty understanding English. In particular, Alina learned that in a week representatives of the European Community, the President of the United States, and representatives from Saudi Arabia and Kuwait were going to have an important meeting, on which great hopes were pinned for a secure peace.

Rita clarified that from the Arab countries there would be no politicians, but private individuals, including the oil magnates who had started all this fuss with the combined Muslim detachments.

"Now," added Rita, "everyone hopes that at this meeting in Vienna all misunderstandings will be clarified and the situation in Europe will finally quiet down. But in Israel everything will not end so soon." Then Rita made a strange grimace, and it was difficult to tell whether she was upset by this or delighted.

It came clear to Alina why she had never felt as free with Rita as with Oksana or even with Marina. The women were on opposite sides of the barricades. The existing situation was in Rita's favor, as it gave her the opportunity to live in Europe, and most importantly, to be with Khalid. The end of the war, the ability to return to Israel—all that Alina so passionately desired—would herald a difficult situation for Rita, not only because of her husband, but more ominously because she was living with the enemy, and if the war ended, Khalid would be held accountable for his participation in it.

As often happens in life, everything seemed to resolve itself in one day. Alina went to visit Jacques one day, and after dinner, Jacques, who still treated Alina quite reservedly, was buoyant with triumph. It turned out that he had managed to contact Alina's husband and had received an email from him. Jacques inspiredly announced his achievement, forgetting to simplify his English, but Alina was able to gather that in America, at the very beginning of the war, the Americans had created a website where all people who lost contact with Israelis could send their messages. The website also served as a source of information about the upcoming conference in Vienna.

Earlier that morning, an employee of the Greek Embassy had phoned Alina to inform her that they finally had an answer to her inquiry: the boy was indeed in a Russian monastery, but only "a male relative or someone who had a power of attorney certified by a lawyer could come for him."

Jacques was going to try to help Alina communicate all of this in English in an email to her husband—since there were no Cyrillic fonts available—but without the slightest hesitation Alina eagerly began to write everything in Russian, albeit in Roman script, causing him to grin condescendingly. When she finished the letter, overcoming her usual bashfulness, and not looking back towards Jacques, Alina added: "Ya lublu tebya"—and then ran out into the corridor to hide the tears that spilled from her eyes.

The culmination of this happy day was the appearance of Oksana, who, silently entering the ward, found Alina and Jacques discussing, or rather arguing, whether her husband would be able to leave Israel for Ron. Oksana, who entered with Jacques' back to her, grimaced at Alina threateningly, letting Alina know she felt jealous, but Alina just waved to her friend, for today it was difficult to ruin Alina's mood.

Oksana had been released for lack of evidence, all charges against her had been dropped. The mafia, fortunately for her, turned out to be more powerful than the law in real life—not at all like in Oksana's favorite detective stories. Oksana had become so bold that she had decided she would stay with Jacques in Germany after the war, while asking for a divorce from her husband. The war, according to her, would certainly end after the meeting in Vienna… Jacques happily nodded his head in assent, not particularly caring what Oksana was saying, as he now worked for two large German firms via the Internet and earned enough to support her and Davidik.

Then leaving Oksana alone with Jacques, Alina went to see Gosha, taking some pies to him, along with the good news. She was pleased to see that he felt better today. The crisis he had gone through with a high fever following the course of chemotherapy had passed, and Gosha, reclining in bed and radiant despite his puffy blue eyes, made plans for a trip around the world with Marina, while holding her plump hand in his bony palm. Marina listened patiently and nodded her head seriously to the beat of Gosha's dreams, gently dabbing with a soft napkin the sweat that appeared on his big shaved head.

Alina stepped out into the hospital courtyard, adjacent to a small park. Two tall, spreading spruces guarded a rigid alley of unknown gnarled trees, their black branches without a single leaf, as, incidentally, befitted the time of year. The park was covered with a thin layer of freshly fallen snow, in places stitched with a chain of squirrel footprints that looped between the trunks. The setting sun painted the overall black-and-white vista in watercolor shades of pink. All this Alina had once loved so much…

And where was the heat and dust, palm trees and lizards basking on hot stones; where was the sea, sparingly measuring out some coolness in the evenings; where was the hubbub of a multilingual crowd? Where was it all—all that before had seemed so strange, and had now become so near and dear?

Where was her home?

Epilogue (a year later)

THE FRIENDS WERE SITTING in a café by the seashore—the very southern sea that Alina had yearned for in Germany. The winter day in Israel was wonderful, warm and clear. The sun was shining, not burning, just warming; the cool air was saturated with the smell of algae. The sea was slightly stormy. A slight hum was heard from the tables, accompanied by the characteristic rustle of rolling pebbles rubbing against the sand.

The few visitors to the café were talking quietly, as if afraid to drown out the whisper of this huge—sometimes formidable, sometimes affectionate—creature, who was sucking up to people on this clear day with the sound of his surf.

Oksana, who had flown in from Munich the day before for her divorce proceedings, did not take her eyes off the sea, blue with greenish streaks and silver foam, until Alina got angry and changed seats with her, so that Oksana's back was to the sea:

"Look at me! Tell me!" Alina chastised.

Oksana raised her eyes, the color of which exactly mimicked the shade of the sea shimmering behind her. "Yes, a lot has happened this year. Gosha, you know, passed away a month after your departure. A week before his death, he handed over ten thousand dollars to Marina. He was in his right mind and thinking clearly, and he did this in the presence of me and Jacques. But more remarkably, it turns out that he had already ordered and bought 2 tickets for a round-the-world cruise. It would have been unprofitable to return them, since almost the entire amount would have been lost. So Marina and Dana circled the globe in a first-class cabin on an ultra-modern liner. And not far from the shores of New Zealand, which Gosha had so dreamed of seeing, Marina, the unyielding and stoic Marina, threw Gosha's ring and a bundle of his letters to her into the sea, as he had asked."

"Did Gosha write letters?"

"Imagine—a letter every day. It even seemed to me that some were poems, but Marina did not volunteer much... Somehow Gosha's wife found out about the money and about the trip, and she wanted to destroy Marina. Marina had to hire a lawyer to represent her in court, and I'm afraid that all Gosha's money went towards that.

"Marina had parted with Victor, it turns out, even before the war, but she is a proud woman, that Marina. So she didn't tell anyone about this—not even you, when you were held hostage together at the school. She had caught him on one of the night shifts when she had unexpectedly brought Dana to the hospital with a high fever. Mostly, she had been offended that Victor had not only cheated on her—it had not even been with a nurse, but with a nurse's assistant. This she could not forgive. So she took Dana out of Israel on our ship—the one that did not explode. When they returned to Israel, the girl flatly refused to live with her father, since she had become attached to Marina, as she has no mother. So she lives with Marina, and Victor gives them money.

"And Rita, your friend, stayed with Khalid in Germany. He was charged with war crimes and placed under house arrest."

"I know," Alina lit a second cigarette. "Rita came to Israel, came to me: she asked me to testify at the trial that Khalid did not mock the hostages and, in general, had ended up joining the combined Muslim detachments in order to save Rita. Believe me, I really didn't want to get involved in this, but I told her that I understood that I had debts that must be repaid."

"Now about my family," Oksana straightened her back. "Vlad returned to Romania with his friend—also, it turns

138

out, a Romanian emigrant. They have jointly opened the Blue Moon café in Bucharest, right next to the central casino. With that theme they went big: a cinema, guest rooms, disco. Vlad turned out to be a skillful businessman—even better than Michal, remember him? Now Vlad is using all his legal knowledge to formalize his relationship with his black-browed friend and adopt a child, since there are many orphans in Romania.

"By the way, about Michal. He and his wife adopted—you will not believe this—four children. I tell you, there are enough orphans… And Sofia is in Israel, you know?"

"No," Alina was upset that Sofia had not tried to meet with her. "I only know that Yoram died a hero, trying to resist either terrorists or marauders who penetrated the base. You know, at his age, such a heroic and quick death is a gift from above."

"I don't know," Oksana averted her eyes, as if embarrassed by Alina's pathos, "I don't think that death at any age or in any form can be considered a gift. Everything that you were, your very being, is destroyed. But what can I say … on such a sunny day with a blue sky, amid the sound of the surf and the cries of the seagulls, I don't want to talk about death…

"So," continued Oksana, "Sofia, having learned about the death of Yoram, decided that her son needed to be raised in the country where his father lived, despite the fact that he is not a Jew according to Israeli laws, and she came here, converted, and had Jonathan circumcised. Now she works for some Romanian Jews, running a household.

"And most importantly, Yoram's daughters have become attached to Sofia, you know how she is… They visit her, invite her to visit, she takes their children for the weekend and walks with them—she's like a real grandmother! Jonathan goes to a very good school, as Yoram left money for tuition and everything else. Sofia sold the house in Brashevo, and with this money, we will be doing Jacques' third operation in a week, at which point he should get back on his feet completely." Joy and anxiety flashed in Oksana's eyes.

"Don't be afraid," Alina tried to dispel Oksana's fear that Jacques, having freed himself from disability, would want to free himself from her. "Then everything will be even better! He will not need to prove anything to anyone, and he will just love you…"

"God willing," Oksana sighed and thought for a minute, then continued, "Katya and Dzhabril are in Libya. They work a lot. Katya, of course, is happy—she helps people. And Dzhabril is saving money, since he wants to go to America with Katya, and take her children there. And Jacques and Davidik and I, if we can, will stay in Germany. And my girls will complete their army service and then come to us."

"Have you seen David?"

"I tried… He didn't want to. He cursed me on the phone, screaming terribly."

"How strange. With me he cried so violently…"

The friends were silent. It was difficult and inconvenient to talk about this topic. Oksana didn't even defend herself. "Okay," she finally shrugged, as if to drive away the unpleasantness, "you didn't tell me how Ron was found."

How was Ron found? Carefully, as if afraid to accidentally open the just-healed wound, Alina told Oksana the last part of their tale.

Alina's husband was able to get permission from the army to fly to Athens, and told Alina and Mashenka to meet him there. They spent the night at the Hilton, where her husband was very surprised that Mashenka was nodding to the doormen as if they were old acquaintances. In the morning they flew to Thessaloniki together and, leaving the "girls" in the hotel, the husband went to Athos to get a permit to visit the monastery at the pilgrim center, as this was the only way to get into the monastery.

A few hours later, Alina received a surprising phone call from the same pilgrim center, and was officially asked, on behalf of the abbot of the monastery, to come, despite the fact that women were not allowed to visit Athos.

It turned out that the monk that Louise had met was actually the abbot of the monastery, and Ron had been under his personal patronage all this time.

And to think that on the very days when Alina and Mashenka had been senselessly wandering around Athens, warming up in hotel lobbies, Father Konstantin, which was the name of the abbot, and Ron had been in the capital on the abbot's business, and had lived for a week in a boarding house at a church which was literally on the next street over from Alina's then refuge! No wonder she had looked searchingly at each child, convinced that Ron was walking somewhere along the neighboring streets.

And now this blue-eyed, Leo Tolstoy-like monk, in his melodious pre-revolutionary Russian (which further increased his resemblance to the pillar of Russian literature), was telling her about the extraordinary abilities of her boy, who, seeing his mother, gripped her with a stranglehold and, embarrassed to cry fully, whined softly, burying himself in her knees.

It was impossible to predict how these several months spent in an Orthodox monastery would affect her son in the future, but never before that day had Alina, who had always been skeptical of religion and clergy, come so close to believing in God as at that moment, when, speechless from excitement and overwhelming gratitude, she had pressed her lips to the hand of Father Konstantine as he extended it in parting.

The last thing Alina told Oksana about was how the ship they returned from Greece on by sea had moored in the Haifa port. Alina had suddenly felt scared. Everything was the same as it had been then: the square in front of the port was densely filled with people... Alina had closed her eyes for a minute—it had seemed to her that she again heard the guttural cries of the Mujahideen.

Alina had shaken her head, driving away the obsession. This could not be: the combined squads had gone back to Saudi Arabia; agreements had been signed. Her fingers squeezed her husband's warm palm tightly.

Their reunion had not been as it should have been. They had not been alone for a minute, even at night. Now, in his reciprocal gentle squeeze, she felt the expectation and hope for the real union of their love. Nearby, clutching the handrails, their children tried to pull themselves up to peer over the rails, as they shouted joyfully. Squinting, Alina made out in the crowd her older boys, and her parents—of course, they could not sit at home. Like the commander on a morning round up line, Alina mentally calculated the people before her: everything was in place. Despite war, separation, death, everything was here, all together.

Life goes on...

www.ingramcontent.com/pod-product-compliance
Lightning Source LLC
Chambersburg PA
CBHW050410030726
47503CB00006B/2119

* 9 7 8 1 9 5 0 3 1 9 9 6 1 *